Lonnie, Me, and. . . .

Books and stories by Marian Allen

Novels
SAGE Book 1: The Fall of Onagros
SAGE Book 2: Bargain With Fate
SAGE Book 3: Silver and Iron
Sideshow in the Center Ring
A Dead Guy at the Summerhouse

Short Story Collections
Lonnie, Me and the Hound of Hell
Turtle Feathers
The King of Cherokee Creek
MA's Monthly Hot Flashes: 2002-2009
Other Earth, Other Stars
Shifty

Visit the author at
http://MarianAllen.com

Lonnie, Me, and. . . .

Marian Allen

Per Bastet

Lonnie, Me, and. . . .

Copyright © 2018 Marian Allen

Published by Per Bastet Publications LLC, P.O. Box 3023 Corydon, IN 47112

Cover art by T. Lee Harris

ISBN 978-1-942166-40-5

Dedicated to Ruth Genarose Turner,
who liked Lonnie best.

Lonnie, Me,
and. . . .

Contents

Marian Allen

Lonnie, Me, and the Hound of Hell

My wife and Lonnie's wife leant against the back door with their arms crossed over their chests and that blank look they always get when they're trying to decide whether to laugh or rip us new ones.

They didn't know yet what happened — come to that, neither did I.

First I knew of any of it was when I opened his tool shed door and saw him throw something into a bucket of fire. The flame *foomphed* up and I grabbed his shirt-tail and hauled backwards, both of us going ass over tip just before the whole shed went *ka-blooie*. Now we were explaining things to the cops.

"It was an accident," I said. I'm a big guy — bigger than Lonnie, bigger than the tall cop, three times bigger than the short cop — and my voice rumbles. Naturally, everybody calls me Tiny.

"Yeah. It ain't like him and me are terrorists." Lonnie did that head-bobbing silent chuckle that meant he thought he was being funny. He waved at the girls and called, "Hey there, Mrs. Terrorist and Mrs. Other Terrorist."

"He was making wine," I said, which was pure meanness. Lonnie's wife, Leona, is a hardshell Baptist. She would come closer to countenancing a terror bomb or a deal with the Devil than she would Lonnie making liquor.

After the cops left, Leona said, "Mary Lee and me'll make some lemonade while you two desperados clean up the yard."

Lonnie and me sorted the splinters from the shovels, gradually getting used to the idea of there not being a building there any more. We could hear the girls inside the kitchen, laughing, but we've both been married long enough to know that didn't mean there wasn't ever going to be trouble about it. I was probably in the clear, personally, since I only came into it at the last minute, but I expected to hear Mary Lee sing a couple choruses of "What you and Leona see in that Lonnie is beyond me."

It's beyond me, too, most of the time, but the four of us went through school together, from nursery school on up. When you've known somebody that long, you don't have to see anything in them.

And that's when the hound showed up.

He came stiff-legging around the house with his head down and his nose up, shoulders hunched and tail tucked. He was about the size of a beagle, but high-rumped, barrel-chested and long in the shanks. His hair was black, glinting red where the sun struck off it, kind of medium-long and slicked down to his skinny body. His ears stuck up in points. He had a length of chain around his neck in place of a collar, cinched so tight it's a wonder he could swallow.

"That dog ain't none of yours, is it?" Lonnie asked. "I never seen it over at your place."

Mary Lee and me lived across the street. If I'd got a new dog, Lonnie would have known it before I did, so he wasn't really asking, he was just pointing out something we both knew.

"No, it ain't mine. If I had a dog that looked that bad, I'd make it wear a paper bag over its whole self."

Leona and Lonnie's Maine Coon Cat, a twenty-pound porker named Rocky, jumped off the back porch to investigate. The dog focused on him and gave a throaty snarl, his hackles and back hair standing up till he looked like a warthog. Rocky went up a tree so fast, we didn't see him stop to climb it.

I felt my jaw drop. Rocky feared neither man nor beast, but there he was, treed like a fluffy kitten with a pink bow around its neck.

Lonnie picked up a chunk of wood from the debris pile and chucked it at the mongrel.

The dog caught the chunk. Then, real slow, he shambled over to Lonnie and dropped it.

Lonnie goggled at the wood, then at the dog, then at me. He pointed a trembling finger at the dog's toothmarks. "Lookit that! Scorched!"

I looked. "Lonnie, damn near every piece of wood that's left from outta that shed is scorched. What are you saying?"

The girls brought us some lemonade and went back in. Lonnie and me sat in lawn chairs on the concrete slab where the shed used to be and Lonnie explained, eying the dog the whole time.

"You remember we read that story, back in school?"

"Some of us read more than one, buddy."

"Ha, ha. I mean that one where the guy sells his soul to the Devil and gets all kinds of good luck?"

"Yeah, right up until Old Scratch came to collect."

Lonnie waved a sooty hand. "Got him a good lawyer and wiggled out of it. If it would'a' been me, I'd put Leona up against him. That little gal could argue the smell off a skunk." He lifted his lemonade glass in a proud salute to his wife. "But, anyways, I got to thinking, like, about time-share condos." He sat back, sipping, wiggling his eyebrows.

I didn't get the connection. And then I did.

"You got to thinking you could sell the Devil . . . a time-share of your soul?"

"Two minutes." He leaned forward, forearms on his knees, and winked. "Get it, buddy? 'The Greatest Two Minutes in Horse Racing', right? I bet on the longest shot in the Kentucky Derby, the Devil makes my horse win — for real, no fair making him win and then he gets caught for doping and gets disqualified or nothing like that. And the Devil gets my soul for two minutes after I die."

"What's in it for him, if it turns out you're going to hell anyway?"

"Well, that's just his tough luck. Besides, I'm saved. This would be a pure two-minute business transaction. But. . . ."

"It didn't work?"

Lonnie flopped a hand at the four walls that weren't around us. "You seen what happened. Just when he popped up out of the fire, everything went *blammy*."

"Yeah, it — What do you mean, 'Just when he popped up'?"

"I seen him, didn't you?"

"No."

"Well, ol' Lonnie seen him. Kind of seen him. I think. But then you grabbed me and everything blew up. By the way, thanks, buddy. You hadn't jerked my tail, I'd'a been toast. I owe you. You name it, it's yours."

I couldn't think of anything Lonnie had that I wanted, except my hedge clippers back, but they'd been in the shed, and they might be in Kingdom Come or up the tree with Rocky.

Speaking of which, Rocky *merowwed* and the dog *whuffed* up at him.

Lonnie said, "You ever hear such language from a innocent animal? Tiny — I believe this dog is Old Nick's. I mean, *look* at it! Sweet Jesus!"

The mutt *huffed* and grumbled, and ambled around past the carport and into the alley.

"You see that? You see how the name of the Lord drove him hence?"

"He just got bored because you didn't throw the stick again."

"No. No, he — What's this?" Lonnie snagged another

chunk of wood and prodded a piece of paper on the concrete between us. "It flew out when that hell-hound shook itself."

I picked up the paper. It was covered in bristly black hairs, and it was folded skinny and creased in the middle, like it had been tucked through a link in the dog's chain-link collar.

I unfolded it and read aloud:

"This dog is yours."

From back behind the carport, here come the clang of a garbage can going over.

"Lord of the Flies," Lonnie moaned, and I had to help him in.

~*~

The phone rang in the middle of the night. I checked the clock: just a little before three. My heart thudded like it always does when the phone rings after ten. *Momma? Grandpa? Mary Lee's sister, changing her mind about her wallpaper?*

It was Lonnie, whispering so Leona couldn't hear him.

"Tiny? That dog is outside. He's been out there, barking and whining and howling since dead midnight. I woke up and looked out the window and seen him down in the back yard. He looked up at the window here, and his eyes is glowing red!"

"That's how dogs' eyes do when the light hits them at night, Lon. Go back to bed."

"How can I go back to bed, with that hell-hound prowling around out there?"

"Did Rocky ever come down out of the tree?"

"Yeah, he come down and come in, and he won't go out. Oh, Lordy, I wish I'd never thought of that deal! Now the Devil's gone and dumped this Beast on me that's too mean for perdition! That's what I get for rattling the Devil's cage. It just serves me right. Oh, I am so sorry. Oh, what in the world am I going to do?"

I had my serious doubts that, if the Devil was going to dump a dog, he'd leave a note, especially not on paper, which is kind of well known for catching on fire. But Lonnie wasn't in any state for logical arguments, so I said, "Make some holy water and sprinkle it around the doors and windows. He can't get you, then."

"Oh, yeah!" I could hear Lonnie thumping down the steps and wondered why he bothered to whisper. If Leona could sleep through that elephant stampede, she wasn't likely to wake up if he yodeled, much less spoke out loud. Then he said, "Tiny?"

"Yeah?"

"How do you make holy water?"

"You take some water. . . ."

"Yeah?"

"And you boil the hell out of it."

There was silence.

"Swear to God. Some Catholic told me." Okay, he told me as a joke, but Lonnie didn't need nothing but comfort. This would give him something to do and make him feel better, and it wouldn't hurt anything. Unless. . . . "Let the water cool down before you stick your fingers in it to fling it around."

"Oh, yeah — Important safety tip. Thanks, buddy. You're a life-saver!"

"Yeah." I felt a little ashamed of myself, but I was too sleepy to back out of it.

On the other end of the phone, Lonnie ran water into a metal pan. "Listen, the girls are going shopping tomorrow, so you come over when Mary Lee does, okay?"

"Okay."

"Okay, Tiny?"

"Okay!"

"Come over for breakfast. About nine. Okay?"

"Okay. Nine o'clock."

I wrote a PostIt note telling Mary Lee about the breakfast invitation, stuck it to her eyeglasses and crawled in beside her.

I've got this smoky green coffee mug that was my daddy's and his daddy's before him. It got a crack in it, somewhere down the line, but it's too heavy to come all the way apart. Lonnie's kind of like that sometimes: he gets these cracked notions, and he's too thick to break him of them. I didn't sleep worth a damn, expecting the phone to ring every minute with Lonnie throwing some kind of chicken fit about the dog, but I finally drifted off.

~*~

Next morning, the girls only stayed long enough to make sure we got the dishes the right way in the dishwasher before they took off. Lonnie watched out the front picture window until the car turned the corner, then motioned me into the kitchen and onto the back porch.

The mongrel was stretched out on his side on the grass, sound asleep in the sun. His forepaws and muzzle were coated with dirt, where he'd been digging somewhere.

"Last night," Lonnie said, "I done like you told me and sprinkled that holy water around the doors and windows. And this morning, Leona found the pan of water on the table and asked me what it was. And I said I was going to boil some eggs last night but changed my mind. And she opened up the back door and flang the water out, and that hell-hound was standing out there and the water went all over him and he yelped like he was scalded, and run off. Now, what do you think of that?"

I thought that I would have yelped and run if somebody had thrown a pan of water on me out of the clear blue sky, but I could see that Lonnie wasn't in the mood to be sensible. I didn't answer him, just stood on the porch and stared at the dog. I don't generally say a lot, so Lonnie let me alone. After a while, he went in and got us both some coffee and an Oreo apiece and we parked our butts on the porch rail and dunked and slurped and thought.

Finally, I put down my cup on the windowsill and said, "There's only one thing to do, Lon."

"What?"

"We're going to have to baptize that dog."

When a man has a headache, he takes an aspirin. When a man is certain sure he's done a service to raise Old Nick, it stands to reason giving equal time to the other side would cancel it out. But would Lonnie think so? That was the question.

Lonnie looked back and forth between the mutt and me. "Sprinkle or dunk?" he asked.

"Well, sprinkling'd be easier."

"But dunking's surer. I know Leona wouldn't count sprinkling."

I nodded. "Dunking it is. You still got that washtub in the cellar? The one we bobbed for apples in last Christmas?"

"Sure do. Right down where you helped me put it away."

"Hose hooked up to the side spigot?"

"Yep."

"Okay. You fix some more of that holy water and I'll bring the tub up and run it full of the regular stuff. But first, I'm going to go across home and get a couple of things."

Over at my house, I grabbed a bottle of dog shampoo, so if the neighbors saw us we could say we was giving the dog a bath, and a heavy chain leash. Back at Lonnie's, I fastened one end of the chain around Leona's metal wash-line pole and snapped the other end onto the mongrel's collar-chain before he knew what was happening. He came awake when I hooked him up, and I pulled my hands away, thinking about that snarl he'd given old Rocky yesterday. All he did was roll his head back and look at me upside down and give his tail a couple of thumps against the ground. When he did that, I knew what it was I had to do. I didn't like it, and Mary Lee wasn't going to like it, but that was the way it was going to be. But I had to do this, first.

When Lonnie came back out with Leona's spaghetti pot full of steaming water, I had the washtub on the grass and half-way full from the outside tap. I nodded at the tub, and Lonnie poured the hot water in.

I unbuttoned my shirt and skinned it off, but I left on my undershirt. The neighbors were going to get enough of a show as it was.

The mutt knew something was up. He slunk away as far as the chain would let him go and laid down on his belly, his head on his forepaws and his eyes on us.

"He don't like that holy water," Lonnie said. "He don't like that at all. Say, don't we need a preacher or something?"

"You want to tell a preacher you raised a hell-hound when you tried to sell two minutes of your soul to the Devil? Besides, this is in the nature of an emergency, and anybody can baptize in an emergency."

Lonnie nodded.

I hunkered down and snapped my fingers. "Come on, fella," I crooned. "Come on. Ol' Tiny ain't gonna hurt you. You know that, don't ya?"

The dog raised his eyebrows and whined.

"You can't just call a fiend," Lonnie said. "You gotta abjure 'em."

I cocked my head up at him. "Okay, give me that again."

"I seen it in a movie. You gotta say, like, 'I abjure thee, by all that's holy, to come.' Like that."

"Well, you're the expert." I turned back to the dog, feeling like a fool. "I abjure thee, by all that's holy, to come on, boy. Come on."

The mutt belly-crawled over and stuck his grubby nose under my hand.

"Atta boy. Good boy." I scooped him up and lowered him into the water.

He made a lunge for the other side of the washtub, but I grabbed his collar. He thrashed and plunged and scrabbled against the sides of the tub.

"Hold him, Tiny!" Lonnie yelled. "Hold him!"

"Well, don't help me or nothing!" I shouted back. The damned dog was about to dislocate my shoulder and we were both soaked to the skin. He was a strong son-of-a-gun, but he knew I was stronger. He stopped trying to go sideways and tried rearing up like a horse. "Calm down, now," I said, though I guess it was more an order than a suggestion. "Calm down."

"Say the words!" Lonnie hollered.

"What do you think I'm doing, quacking like a duck? Stop yelling. You're scaring him."

"Say the baptizing words!"

I started to, then realized we had forgotten a pretty important feature.

"What am I gonna baptize him as?"

"As? You gonna baptize him as a dog!"

"I mean his name. You can't get baptized without a name."

"Well, think one up. You're his God-father, ain't you?"

The dog rolled his eyes at me, jerking and shivering. As soon as I relaxed, he made a dive for the edge.

"Homer!" I bellowed, pulling him back and shoving him under three times quick. "I baptize thee, in the name of the Father and of the Son and of the Holy Ghost, HOMER!" I hefted him out and set him on the grass.

He stood there, breathing hard, feet splayed out like he couldn't believe he was back on dry land. Then he hauled off and gave a good, long shake, throwing water from porch to carport. When he was finished, he sat on his haunches and looked smug.

"Dang!" Lonnie ran a hand over his dripping face.

I grabbed my shirt and dried off with it as best I could, then passed it to Lonnie. "How about a lemonade? I reckon we earned it."

"Two lemonades, coming right up."

While he was inside, I emptied the washtub and ran the spaghetti pot full of fresh water and took it over to Homer to drink. He lapped it up like he'd dried himself from the inside out.

When Lonnie brought the lemonades, I said, "That's two you owe me, buddy."

He nodded. "I reckon so."

"And I'm calling in my debts, right now."

He looked at me sideways. That wasn't how we did things. We was always owing each other for this or that, but we never kept track of it. He wasn't going to argue with me about it, though. "Okay."

"First, the two minutes you was going to deal to the Devil. I want 'em."

"Say what?"

"I want those two minutes. Any time I say, you do me two minutes of time. That way, if Old Scratch ever shows up and claims you owe him two minutes, you tell him he can't have them 'cause you gave them to me."

Lonnie grinned, his Adam's apple bobbing. "Yeah! Yeah, you got it! Tiny, you are a pure genius! What's the other thing you want?"

I nodded at Homer. "I want that dog."

"You what?"

"I saved him. I want him."

"No." Lonnie shook his head nearly as hard as Homer had. "That dog is going to the pound. That dog is getting put out of my misery."

"I'm claiming that dog, Lonnie. I done baptized that dog, fair and square. He ain't a hell-hound no more."

So this was it. The big showdown, me against Old Nick for the mind — such as it is — of Lonnie Carter.

Lon and Homer eyeballed one another. Lonnie took a big swig of lemonade and Homer lapped up a couple tonguefuls of water. Then Lonnie said, "S'pose the Devil comes and wants him back?"

"The Devil ain't going to want that dog," I said. "That dog's been washed in the blood of the Lamb."

Homer picked that minute to bark.

"See?" I said. "Homer agrees with me. Don't you, boy?"

Homer trotted over and licked my hand.

"Well, now," said Lonnie. "If that don't beat all. Yeah, okay, buddy, you got it. And, Tiny? Thanks."

~*~

I was right — Mary Lee didn't like it any better than I did. We already had two dogs, a big mutt and a little mutt, and neither one of us was crazy about the idea of feeding a middle-sized mutt, too. But Homer turned out to be the sweetest-natured dog that ever lived, once he grew up enough to get some manners. Even Leona and Lonnie's cat Rocky come to like him: Rocky would curl up against him and nap in the cold weather.

"But 'Homer'?" Mary Lee said. "Where did you come up with 'Homer'?"

"Short for Home-Made Sin, which he's ugly as," I said. "Sort of a Nick-name, you might say."

Lonnie, Me, and
the Battle of St. Crispin's Day

It all started when Lonnie got on Facebook. One minute, me and him were chuckling at his wife, Leona, and my wife, Mary Lee, for being "Face-heads", and the next minute, he's on there himself.

Not that he told me. The first I knew of it, Mary Lee whooped, "Oh! I don't believe it!" from the little room where she keeps the computer and her sewing machine. Then she stood in the doorway like she was leaning on it for support and said, "Guess who just friended me on Facebook."

"Lady Goo-goo."

"Lady Gaga, and no. Lonnie Carter."

"Lonnie Carter? *Our* Lonnie Carter? Across the street Lonnie Carter? What in the world is Lonnie doing on there?"

"Ask him yourself," she said. "He's on here now."

She ducked back into The Hole, waving to me to follow, but I'm built like a linebacker — maybe a little gone to seed — and no way would there be room in there for me, much less me and Mary Lee and a computer and a sewing machine. I grabbed my Bigman husky-plus jacket and hot-footed across the street.

Leona opened the back door before I knocked. When I asked her where Lonnie was, she grinned like a polecat and pointed toward the living room.

And there he sat, holding some kind of little something in his long skinny knobby hand and poking at it with one finger, looking as serious as if he was working.

"Hey, buddy," I said.

He jumped so hard, the thing flew up out of his hands and tumbled through the air. He snatched at it but missed and the thing landed *plump* on the couch cushion beside him.

"Dang it, Tiny!" He grabbed the thing and rubbernecked between inspecting it for damage and glaring up at me. "I coulda broke my smart phone!"

I would have thought giving Lonnie Carter a smart phone was about like giving a banana to a cat, but he sat me down and showed it off and seemed to know how to work it.

"And you know," he said, "you and me has had some laughs about this Facebook thing, but Leona got me onto it and who do you think friended me?"

"Lady Goo-ga."

Leona came in with a cup of coffee for each of us, said, "Lady *Goo*-ga?" and went back into the kitchen.

I gave up. "Well, who was it?"

"Daniel Halloran."

"Daniel. . . . Daniel. . . ." The name was ringing a bell, somewhere in there. "*Danny* Halloran? Dime-Store Danny? King of the Five-Finger Discount?"

"That's the one! And guess what he's doing?"

"Ten to twenty for grand larceny?"

"No, he's a priest! Father Dan is what they call him. And guess where he's priesting?"

Lonnie r'ared back on the couch and bobbed his head in encouragement, but I was all done guessing for the day. "I don't know, Lonnie. Tell me."

"Saints Crispin and Crispinian. And guess what day it's getting to be."

It was a day I hadn't thought of for over twenty years, but Lonnie had harked me back, and I knew right away what he meant.

"St. Crispin's Day," I said.

If you have a Catholic church in your neighborhood — at least, if you had one when Lonnie and me were growing up — and if it was named after a saint, you had a festival on or around that saint's day every year. Saints Crispin and Crispinian, being twins, had the same feast day, but everybody just called it St. Crispin's Day for short.

"And Danny invited us back."

"Say what?"

"St. Crispin's Day, Tiny. October 25. The festival's this Saturday."

~*~

So the next thing I know, I'm heading across town, back to the old neighborhood, with Lonnie running off at the mouth about stuff I'd just as soon forget. The only good thing was that Mary Lee wasn't there to hear some of it. We'd invited the wives to come along, but Leona's hardshell Baptist family had always boycotted Pagan festivals, and Mary Lee didn't want to go without Leona.

"Happy days," Lonnie kept saying. "Good days."

It made my hair stand on end.

"How'd you talk Leona into letting you off the leash?" Not that Mary Lee and me have some kind of open marriage or anything, but Leona keeps a sharper eye on Lonnie than Mary Lee does on me. In fact, Mary Lee says the only thing about me that gives her any cause for concern is hanging around with Lonnie. But that's just talk. Her and Leona live in each other's pockets; it would break either one of them's heart if Lonnie and me stopped being friends.

Lonnie winked in answer to my question and said, "Trust ol' Lonnie." He patted my shoulder, like that would reassure me. I figured what he meant was, Leona was counting on me to keep him out of trouble. From the way he had one ankle crossed over his knee, foot wiggling, fingers twiddling on his legs, it looked like I was going to have my day cut out for me.

Before I knew it, we were driving along streets that looked kind of familiar but no kind of familiar. A lot of houses and businesses were exactly where and how I remembered, but some were missing, some were wrecks, some had siding instead of the wood they were born with. Some trees were bigger than I remembered, and some were stumps. Lena's grocery had a big BODEGA sign on it and the window in the side of the building where we used to line up for snow-cones said "*fruteria*" over it.

Sts. Crispin and Crispinian hadn't changed, though. Still big and Gothic in the front, with brick additions straggling out behind it. The street that ran in front of it was barricaded off for two blocks in either direction for the festival.

"I was forgetting about that," I said. The last time we were around for St. Crispin's Day, neither one of us could drive, not to mention that we could walk to it from where we lived.

Lonnie pulled out that phone of his and started giving me directions.

"How does that thing know how to go?"

"It's got a map on it, see?"

After I didn't hit a lamppost and a garbage can while Lonnie had his phone up my nose, I followed his directions and got around the blockade and into the rectory parking lot.

Lonnie did a few more *beeps* and *boops* on his phone and unfolded his long skinny self out of my car.

I reached up and picked a dry brown catalpa pod off the tree above us.

"Remember the time we tried smoking these things?"

A big voice boomed, "I prefer cigars these days, and I'm trying to cut down on those."

The big voice belonged to a tubby priest with a round red nose, bright blue eyes and thinning strawberry blond hair.

If Lonnie hadn't told me who we were meeting, I would never have known him.

16

"Danny? Dang, Dime-Store! Long time!"

"Tiny! Weasel!"

We wrung each other's hands and slapped each other's shoulders and stood around laughing with our hands in our pockets until a thin old woman opened the back door.

"Tea's getting cold, Father Dan."

We followed Danny through the kitchen and down a hall into a cluttered and comfortable sitting room that might have belonged to any normal bachelor. Well, except that there was a tray on the coffee table with a teapot on it, and tea cups and a bowl of sugar lumps and a tray of cookies.

When the old lady had closed the door behind herself, Lonnie put on a high voice and said, "May I have two lumps of sugar, Miss Halloran?"

Danny shook a fist and said, "Two lumps upside the head, Weasel!"

"Folks don't call me that no more, Dime-Store. I'm just plain Lonnie, now."

"Folks don't call me Dime-Store, either, you know."

Lonnie said, "Naw, it's *Father* Dime-Store, these days."

"I'm still Tiny," I said, and they both laughed.

Danny reached around to a cabinet behind his chair and pulled out a bottle of Beam. He tipped some into his own cup and held the open neck toward ours. "Touch of Kentucky?"

"I married me a hardshell Baptist," Lonnie said. Then he winked and said, "But what the little woman don't know won't hurt me."

I waved the bottle off. Not that I don't drink — I just don't like whiskey.

"I'm saving myself for the beer garden," I said. "You do still have a beer garden, don't you?"

That set Lonnie back off on the "happy days" magical memory tour about how us boys would sneak into the festival's beer garden and drink the leftovers and get sick.

Yeah, I really wanted to relive those moments. It's a wonder we didn't catch AIDS or diphtheria or something.

After we finished the tea and whatnot, Danny led us on through the rectory and out the front door, down the walk and out the gate and maybe twenty years back in time.

There were a lot of new faces, and a lot of older faces that used to be younger. Everybody who remembered us was glad to see us — or pretended they were, anyway. Our old friends' mothers seemed to get a charge out of telling us how great their kids were doing now, implying that our moving out of the neighborhood was the best thing that ever happened to it.

All the games were the same. They called the bean bag toss "corn hole" now, for some reason, but it was the same game. Looked like the same equipment, come to that.

Danny strutted around with us, waving at parishioners, laughing at our friends' mothers' jokes about the shines we used to get up to. It didn't take me long to have enough, and I would have been just as happy to go on home, but Lonnie was having a blast, and I didn't have the heart to throw a wet blanket on him.

When we got to the beer garden, I decided not to get a beer, after all. I was hoping to be driving home sooner rather than later, and I had perfectly good beer in my own refrigerator. I reminded Lonnie he was going to be breathing at Leona by and by, and Danny backed me up, so we all three got bratwurst and lemon slush and sat down at a picnic table to take in the passing show.

I'd finished my brat and half my slush when I heard a sound that made my blood run cold: Lonnie giggled. Not just one giggle, like a little burp that surprises you when you swallow water too fast. No, this was a giggle that meant something, like belching "America the Beautiful" on a bet. I swiveled around toward him, and there he was, red in the face, covering his mouth and giggling, tears of laughter squeezed out of the corners of his eyes, and that damned Danny grinning like the cat that ate the canary.

"You didn't," I said. "You did. You underhanded mackerel-snapper; you been spiking his slush for him, haven't you?"

"Oh, what's the harm? You're driving, and I didn't slip it to him unaware — just offered it and poured it where it was wanted."

"Like Lonnie's got any sense."

Danny had the grace to look a little doubtful.

I talked Lonnie into eating his brat, and that steadied him some. Danny probably hadn't given him all that much, but Lon wasn't used to anything but the (very) occasional beer, and he probably felt drunker than he was. He walked okay, talked just a little louder than usual, and thought everything he'd already seen on the way to the beer garden was surprising and wonderful on the way back.

He dug a fold of ones out of his pocket and played every game of chance we passed except the cakewalk. I'd talk him out of playing, then I'd get buttonholed by some hen who'd known my Mom and, when I looked around, Lonnie would be at another one. He won a stuffed panda at the Wheel O' Chance, which he seemed to think Leona would like.

We almost made it. We were right there at the rectory gate when somebody opened the door to the parish hall and a burst of music came out.

"Dancing!" Lonnie shouted. He faked a little tap routine. "Gotta dance! Gotta dance!" He tossed the panda into my arms and loped away from us.

Drinking and gambling and dancing. Leona was purely gonna kill me!

I'm big, but I'm not that fast, and Father Dan couldn't but waddle. By the time we got into the hall, Lonnie had worked his way into the crowd and cut in on a guy who didn't look all too happy about it. The woman he was dancing with was laughing.

I recognized her. Then I recognized the guy.

"Are you kidding me? He's in here two seconds, after twenty years away, and he zeroes in on Jackie the Kipper?" Jacob deKueper, his real name was, but he was "Jackie the Kipper" to us boys, and his big brother, Pete, was "Dutch".

Danny was sweating, and not just from the heat of the parish hall.

"I didn't realize the deKuepers would be here. I haven't seen any of them around for over five years. Jackie must have gotten time off for good behavior."

And the woman.

"Isn't that Yvonne Hargrove Lonnie cut in on?"

"Yvonne deKueper."

"She married the Kipper?"

"She married Dutch."

"This just gets better and better." I craned around, looking for somebody my size but uglier and meaner.

"Surely Dutch won't be here." Danny ran a finger around the inside of his dog collar, then made a twitchy gesture that looked an awful lot like the sign of the cross. "Dutch is still wanted for his part in the hold-up that got Jackie put away."

"I'm gonna go peel Lonnie off that handful of trouble he's dancing with and get going. Thanks for the good time, old pal. If I ever invite you over to my place, take my advice and don't come."

"Sorry, Tiny." His voice faded behind me as I plowed through the dancers.

"Lonnie. . . . Lonnie. . . . Hi, there, Yvonne. Congratulations on your marriage to Dutch."

Lonnie, snockered as he was, let go of her like she'd just grown porcupine spines.

"Dutch? Where? Where's Dutch?"

You know how, in a movie, when somebody asks a question like that, everything gets real quiet, and then you hear an ominous voice saying something like, "He's right here," or "Look behind you," or "Who wants to know?"

Well, Lonnie asked where was Dutch, and then he staggered back and sprawled on the floor, and the world in front of me was filled with a fist.

I'd know that fist anywhere. Those knuckles fit up against my left eye like they were coming home. Somehow, I'd known Dutch would have grown as much as I had, and my automatic return punch tagged him right where I meant it to: above his left eye. Opened the skin of his brow. Didn't do any real damage, but Jackie was, sure enough, still squeamish at the sight of blood, so there was one of Dutch's allies out of commission.

Like always, Dutch hadn't come alone, and one of his cronies picked Lonnie up and threw him toward another guy's fist. Lonnie's legs wouldn't hold him, though, and he reeled out of range.

Women screamed, men shouted, and more than a few folks, overexcited by what Leona would have called the twin devils of drink and dance music, chose up sides and took the opportunity to settle some scores of their own that didn't have thing one to do with Dutch or Lonnie or me.

One bad thing about being big which you might never have thought of, unless you're big, yourself, is that you're kind of hard to miss. Not only can people see you, they can throw a punch in a pretty general direction and still land a hit. And being big doesn't mean a punch doesn't hurt you as much as it hurts a little guy, either.

I'd like to say I gave as good as I got, but I wasn't exactly keeping score. All I can say is, my hands hurt about as much as all the rest of me, so I must have been tagging somebody. At first, it was just my right hand that hurt, and then I realized I was still holding that damn panda. I tried using it for a shield, but Dutch and his boys didn't have a sentimental bone in all their bodies, and they didn't mind punching a stuffed panda any more than they did a person. Then I tried lambasting guys with it, but it didn't even slow them down. By and by, I lost hold of it and it went I knew not where.

All the time, I kept half an ear out for sirens. In my younger days, which I should have remembered, the festival wasn't complete without at least one fistfight breaking out somewhere, though things didn't usually get as general as this one seemed to be. The cops ought to be on the alert, although times had gotten rougher and maybe a mere knock-down drag-out didn't rate anymore.

I could hear Danny's voice, amplified by the sound system, saying, "Boys! Boys! . . .And ladies! A saint's day is no time for violence! Think of the children!" but no sirens.

After what seemed like about three years, when I was backed up against the bingo tables that had been shoved together along the walls, I gave Dutch a good solid wallop and he didn't come back.

Something tugged at my jeans so hard I was afraid my pants would come off, so I took the advice my legs had been giving me for some time and sat down.

"Scrootch on under here, buddy," Lonnie whispered.

I scrootched on under, and there was Lonnie, without a mark on him, with that phone of his out and him *beep*ing and *boop*ing on it to beat the band.

"Lonnie," I said, "what in the ever-lovin' blue-eyed world are you doing?"

"Tweeting with Plaid Girl and L. R. Lee," he said, like that ought to make sense. "They think you're doing great. She said she's going to write you a haiku, and he said for me to take some pictures for him, since he can't be here to take 'em hisself."

"Do I know these people?"

"No."

"Do you know these people?"

"Well, sure."

"I mean in real life."

"Tiny, you just don't get it, do you?"

I figured I'd already got about as much as I could handle. "I guess I don't," I said. "Why don't you just hold onto it for me and I'll get it by and by."

Things sounded like they were sorting themselves out in the world beyond the tables. Danny told everybody to clear the hall until they'd cleaned up and cooled down.

Once everything was nice and quiet, we crawled out. Time teaches wisdom, my mama used to say, and it looked like there was some truth to it. The parish hall hadn't been decorated at all, and the bingo tables had kept flying fists and feet and people out of the windows. The floor was littered with paper and neckties and ball caps and maybe the occasional tooth, but nothing more valuable than that.

"Time to go, buddy," I said.

I almost had him out when he said, "Leona's prize!" We scrounged around and he found it up on the stage, stuffing popping out of its seams and one of its eyes hanging by a thread but, amazingly, no blood on it.

"Somebody's went and blacked both its poor ol' eyes," Lonnie mourned.

"It's a panda, Lon. It comes with black eyes."

I would have told him to leave it but I figured with one hand full of panda and the other full of phone, he couldn't drink anything or play anything or grab ahold of anything, so I let it be.

We left by the back door, heading for the rectory parking lot.

Speaking of two black eyes, by the time we got to the car, both mine were just about swollen shut. I wasn't about to ride in any car Lonnie was driving, with him full of whiskey slush and still plaiding or twitting or whatever he was doing with that damn phone.

But the last sight I saw before my eyes hurt too much to hold them open was Mary Lee, arms crossed, leaning against the driver's-side door.

~*~

It was a swift and silent ride home. Mary Lee drives like she's getting paid for it — not a second wasted, just barely legal. Every time Lonnie started to say something, she said, "No," or, "Hush up," or, "Don't talk or I'll slaughter you." She didn't tell him he couldn't *beedledy-boop* on his phone, though, so there was quite a bit of that.

Leona was waiting for us at our house. Lonnie tucked the phone away and, sliding out of Mary Lee's reach, said, "Honey, I—"

"We'll talk about it at home, you back-sliding reprobate," she said. "Go on and mix yourself up a Alka-Seltzer before you get sick. I'll be right behind you."

"I brung you something."

I forced my eyes open to see how Leona took it.

Lonnie held out that raggedy-butt panda and waggled it so the loose eye flapped around.

"Won it in a game of chance, didn't you? Didn't you?"

Lonnie turned the bear around and looked at it like it was going to give him the answer.

"Home," Leona said.

Lonnie shuffled off home, saying, "C'mon, Chance. You

and me is in the doghouse. Ain't you ashamed of yourself, fighting and all?"

"Leona," I said, "I am so sorry."

"You done your best," she said. She gave me a quick hug and a pat on the shoulder and hugged Mary Lee real big and sniffled.

"Mary Lee," she said, "you two are the best friends ever. I thank the Lord for the both of you." She sniffled again and left.

Mary Lee led me into the kitchen and sat me down. I heard the freezer open and shut and she handed me two bags of frozen peas to hold against my eyes. She put some coffee to brew and sat down across the table from me.

One good thing I'll say about having a friend like Lonnie: Whenever you get in trouble, folks always assume it's his fault. Of course, one bad thing about having a friend like Lonnie is: it usually *is* his fault.

Mary Lee said, "'These wounds I had on Crispin's day.' Remember? That battle speech in *Henry V* that you did in Senior English?"

I hadn't remembered it, but now I did. "Didn't he win? Ol' King Henry?"

"Yes. 'He to-day that sheds his blood with me shall be my brother; be he ne'er so vile.'"

"Is that a fact?"

"You don't remember?"

I said, "I was lucky to remember it long enough to recite it in Senior English." Then I said, "How did you know I needed you? Have we been married that long?"

"I knew because that fool was updating his status on Facebook the whole time. He knows Leona and I are on there. He knows we get his status updates. And yet there he was, posting pictures and going, 'Danny slips me a little Kentucky while Tiny isn't looking. Ha-ha,' and 'Tiny don't want me to have no fun, but I'm a growed man and I know a trick or two.'"

The sheer stupidity of it made me dizzy.

"And then the fight started, and he crawled under some tables and stuck the phone up and snapped pictures and videos. People were rooting for you and sharing the pictures and—" She got up and got us each a cup of coffee.

I took the peas off my eyes and found I could open my peepers enough to see her sweet face.

She said, "Leona was beside herself, so I got Bernadette to run me in and drop me off." Bernadette was the little old lady who lived next door. Feisty little firecracker — I was half-way surprised she didn't wade into the fight instead of just dropping Mary Lee off. She must have had a hair appointment.

The fight was on the local news, and it seems that the guy who pulled Dutch off of me was the cop working the hold-up Dutch was wanted for. The cops had turned up, after all, but they hadn't used their sirens because they didn't want to scare Dutch off.

I called Lonnie — on the regular phone — and Leona let him talk, once she found out it was me calling.

"I'm glad you at least had the sense to call the police with that play-toy of yours."

"I didn't call the police. A man don't call the police to settle his fights for him."

I didn't say it, but I thought, "No, a man crawls under the bingo tables and lets another man settle 'em."

"Naw," Lonnie said. "Somebody on Facebook that had saw Dutch on Local Most Wanted seen the pictures I took, and they called the cops. I ain't no stool pigeon."

"G'night, Lonnie," I said, and hung up the phone real gentle. I went and sat back down next to Mary Lee. "'Ne'er so vile,' huh?" I said. "You know, sometimes I wonder what I see in him, myself."

Lonnie, Me, and the Junkyard of Forbidden Delights

"I got a idea," Lonnie said, which is never something you want to hear, especially when the wives are out of town.

"If it's anything worse than coming over to my house for a couple of beers, forget it." Lonnie and me have been best friends since dirt was new, and the only way I've survived it was by nipping most of his ideas in the bud.

"No, no, Tiny, this'n is good. Just listen. It don't hurt to listen."

My wife, Mary Lee, would have told us both different, but, like I said, she and Lonnie's Leona were out of town at some kind of ladies' convention.

I pushed my chair back and got another mug of coffee. Lonnie had cut half a coffee cake for me from one Leona left him. Lonnie was already most of the way through his half. How he can eat the way he does and still look like a string bean is beyond me. I told Mary Lee once I didn't know where Lonnie put all he eats, and Mary Lee said he probably put it where his brains ought to be.

Lonnie waited until I sat back down, like I couldn't hear without my legs bent. "You listening?"

"I'm listening."

"You know that junkyard out north of town? Scrappy's?"

"The one with the ads that's got a cartoon of a guy in a suit and a car in a slinky red dress, and somebody that can't sing singing about make your old heap happy and take her to Scrappy?"

Lonnie — who can sing, I'll give him that — sang the ad, along with the wink the car in the dress gave at the end.

"What about it?" I knew better than to ask, but it just came out before I thought.

"Well, the guy that owns it isn't really named Scrappy."

"Do tell."

"His real name is Meriweather Fitzbottom."

"Get out and quit lyin'!"

"I know! But that really is his name! Leona knows a gal that works in the recorder's office, and she got it off his property tax bill. Meriweather Fitzbottom, no lie. But that ain't the point. The point is, he's a whatchacallit."

"A junkman?"

"No, that thing Leona's so down on."

"Drinker? Dancer? Gambler? Unitarian Universalist?"

"Dang it, Tiny, be serious! Like Harry Potter."

"Young? English? Wiseass?"

Lonnie's scrawny chicken neck got red, so I knew he was about to lose his temper. That's no fun, so I put half my coffee cake on his plate and said, "Give me another hint. I'm not a very good guesser today."

"You know: a guy that does magic. And don't say magician, 'cause that ain't it."

"Sorcerer? Warlock?"

"That's it!" He slapped me on the shoulder with those long, bony fingers hard enough to raise welts. "He's a warlock."

"You sure you don't mean, like, a Mason or something?"

"No, he's a warlock. Leona said some of the kids in her church youth group come in and said they went to Scrappy's to buy some parts for a car they're fixing up together. Said he was picking something in this garden he has out back of his office shed. They asked him what it was and he told them that good church-going children didn't need to know."

Marian Allen

"What makes you think it was warlockery? Maybe it was marijuana. Or opium. Or heroin. No, you don't grow heroin."

"Heroin comes from horses, don't it?"

Sometimes all you can do with Lonnie is say *yes* and go on. "Yes," I said. "So what makes you think he's a warlock?"

"He told 'em! As good as, anyway. They said he said he had a garden of unearthly pleasures, and they could come back when they were older and he'd fix 'em up."

"Aw, he was just jerking their chains 'cause he knew they were church kids."

"How'd he know, eh?" Lonnie tapped his temple and narrowed his eyes. "Powers!"

I pointed to my eyeballs and said, "20/20 vision. Bet they were wearing their Teens For Jesus t-shirts, like they always do when they run in a pack."

Lonnie got that astonished look he gets when I make sense. "Yeah," he said, "I bet you're right."

I opened my mouth to ask him how he thought the Colts would do this coming season, but he wasn't through worrying that Scrappy bone yet.

"But after Leona told me that, I asked around. You know, at the hardware store and all."

"Ain't that where they moved The Liar's Bench when they remodeled the courthouse square?"

"Well, yeah, but I didn't ask anybody on The Bench."

"Oh. That's okay, then."

"That's what I thought." He winked and tapped the side of his nose, which was his signal for good thinking. "They said Scrappy has a business on the side, selling cures and stuff."

"Cures for what?"

"All kinds of stuff. Warts. Ingrowed toenails." He lowered his voice to a whisper and said, "Man troubles."

I put down my fork and glared.

"I don't mean you got none of that," Lonnie said. "Or me, neither. That's just what they told me at the hardware store."

"So what's your point?"

"Nothing," Lonnie said. "I'm just saying." He picked up our plates and mugs and forks and put them in the sink and ran cold water on them. I was a little bit surprised at Leona; Mary Lee had me trained to rinse my dishes and put them in the dishwasher. I would have thought a hardshell Baptist like Leona would be a better man-trainer than a Methodist like Mary Lee.

Lonnie said, "I was just thinking about Scrappy's because you were wanting to see about a part for that old dryer in your garage. Scrappy's might have what you're looking for."

Now, that was a thought worth thinking. Mary Lee had been after me to haul her old dryer to a junkyard, and I had been arguing that I could fix it and have some charity come pick it up. Not that I'm a saint, but a repair part is a lot easier to load into a truck than a dryer, right?

"Yeah," I said. "They might."

"So why don't we go out there and see?"

"Why do you want to go?"

"I like junkyards."

Well, who doesn't?

"I'll go across and write down what I need and come pick you up."

"Hot dang!" Lonnie clapped his hands together and rubbed them. He was just too darned enthusiastic about this little excursion to suit me, but now I had my heart set on getting that part, and how much trouble could he get in, if I kept an eye on him?

~*~

We were about halfway to Scrappy's when Lonnie stopped playing two-second roulette with the radio and said, "Say, Tiny, did you ever read a book about this guy, Don Juan?"

"Are you back harping on man troubles? Is there something you want to talk to me about, buddy? — Did the girls go off together so Leona could get advice from Mary Lee and you could get advice from me?"

"From *you*?"

I thought the giant, economy-sized load of disbelief he put in those two words was entirely uncalled for.

"Yes, from me!"

"What in the world are you talking about? What's Don Juan got to do with man troubles?"

"He was kind of well-known for not having them."

"He was?"

"The one *I* read about was."

"They must be two of them, then. This one was Mexican or something, and he was like magical. Mushrooms and stuff. I picked up this book about him in the restaurant the other night and read some of it while Leona was in the ladies' room. It was wrote by this guy Carl Castanet or something. That's what got me thinking about Scrappy."

"I don't eat mushrooms, as a rule," I said. "Too squidgy."

"These'ns make you happy." He leaned around so I could see his face — and not as much of the road as I generally like to see — and wiggled his eyebrows.

"Is that what you're going to Scrappy's for? Happy mushrooms?"

"Nah. Something better."

"Better than happy? What — Unearthily pleased from unearthly pleasures?"

He didn't answer.

I risked a glance at him, but he was looking out the side window.

"You better leave them happy mushrooms alone. And everything else he sells besides scrap. You hear me?"

He shrugged.

"Do. You. Hear. Me?"

"I hear you."

"No happy stuff. I'm serious. Okay?"

"Okay, okay!"

I pulled into the scrap yard and turned off the motor.

"Do I need to ask you to wait in the car?" I was seriously regretting letting him come along. Leona kept him on a pretty short leash — which anybody that knew him had to approve. But that meant that, when he took a notion to kick over the traces, he tended to kick 'em good and hard. "I'm here on business," I said. "I catch you happy, I'll clip you one upside the ear."

"I ain't gonna get happy!" He took his pointer fingers and pulled the ends of his mouth down.

"Now ain't that mature?" But I had to laugh, and he punched me on the shoulder and we were friends again.

The instant we cracked open our doors, a couple of them junkyard dogs you hear about came scuttering and barking and growling around the corner of the office shed. They were both big and ugly and bristly and fangy and slobbery and wearing collars studded with spikes, like Mary Lee's middle niece's boyfriend.

We tucked our feet back inside and slammed our doors.

Lonnie said, "Maybe you should have brought Homer."

Homer is my dog, which I got from Lonnie. The fact that Lonnie believes he conjured Homer away from the Devil probably tells you everything you need to know about Lonnie, right there.

A man followed the dogs, shambling along like his feet hurt. He was taller than Lonnie and wider than me, and that made him bigger than an upright freezer. I wondered where he got his coveralls, or if he had to buy a couple bolts of cloth and have them made his size. He was bald as a cue ball, with bushy black eyebrows that were pulled down in a scowl. His eyes were little bitty, and if they'd been any closer together he'd have been a cyclops.

"Down, Cujo," he called in a clear, light tenor.

The dogs dropped to their bellies where they were and laid there, tongues hanging out.

We got out. I had to put my foot down right in front of one of 'em's face. My ankle tingled, just waiting for those teeth to chomp onto it, but the dog acted like I wasn't even there.

Lonnie said, "Which one's named Cujo?"

The man said, "They're both named Cujo."

I was about to get back in the car, but Lonnie was out and had his door closed, so I went around and joined him.

The man's coveralls had "Hi, I'm Scrappy" embroidered over his heart, so I figured this was Meriweather Fitzbottom, himself. I reckoned that if I'd had to go through middle school with a name like that, I'd have two dogs named Cujo, myself.

Scrappy had his arms full. At first, I thought he was cradling a shotgun, but then I saw it was some stems of plants. What Mary Lee calls Money Plant, that smells like cough drops.

"What can I do you fellers for?"

I pulled out the paper where I had what I wanted written down. Scrappy read it and scratched at the heavy black stubble on his chin with a sound like sanding hobnails.

"Yeah," he said, "I got some o' them models back in Section 40L. Back that way." He pointed.

"Do we need a map or something, or is it easy to find?"

"Just straight back that path."

"You go ahead," Lonnie said. "I'll catch you later. I gotta use the can."

He'd been all but dancing in place ever since he got out of the car, so it might not have been a lie. Still, he'd already tipped his hand, and I wasn't about to leave him alone with Scrappy.

"I'll wait for you," I said, giving him the look that meant I was through fooling around.

"Can's around back," Scrappy said. "Go on. It ain't locked. I gotta take these inside."

Lonnie didn't go, but trailed into the shack after Scrappy. I watched from outside as Scrappy put the bundle he was carrying onto the desk, tied it together with string, and tied the string to a nail up near the ceiling. Bundles hung all around the room, covering up the old license plates and hub caps that lined the wall from floor to rafters.

"What's all that stuff for?"

He came out, rubbing his hands on his hips. "This and that."

So maybe Lonnie's hardware store information wasn't completely off base. That wasn't too reassuring.

I didn't like it that I couldn't see around Scrappy's bulk to keep an eye on Lonnie.

"C'mon, Lon," I called. "We don't have all day."

"Sure, we do," Lonnie called back.

"No, you don't," Scrappy said. "I close in twenny minutes. C'mon, I'll show you where you're going."

He shambled off and I had to hustle after him.

Lonnie wasn't long behind us, so I reckoned he'd had him a good quick snoop around and I'd hear all about it on the way home.

But on the way home, all he wanted to do was mess with the part I'd located, and I was busy the whole way keeping him from breaking the dang thing.

~*~

Lonnie and me had a pizza delivered to my house and watched a ball game and cracked a couple of beers, which Leona won't allow in her house. The beers, I mean; she's pretty moderate on the subjects of pizza and sports.

I figured Lonnie had got all that warlock business out of his system, because he never brought it up. Naturally, I wasn't about to.

When I went to bed, I included it in my thank you prayers: *Thank you for Lonnie getting that warlock business out of his system.*

It's enough to make you think God must have a weird sense of humor, because I was deep into a dream where I was turning that washing machine into a red Thunderbird when the phone rang and it was Lonnie.

"Tiny?" His voice was real thin, not like his regular voice at all. "Buddy?"

"Yeah, Lon. What's wrong?"

"I'm in trouble, buddy. Can you come get me?"

"Where you at?" I had an awful thought. Leona would kill me. "Are you in jail?"

"Oh, I wish I was in jail! No, Tiny, I'm on the roof."

"The hell you are!"

"I am. I am. I'm up on the roof."

"The roof of the jail? Was you trying to make a break for it? Never run up, Lon. Don't them movies you watch teach you nothing?"

"Not the jail roof! *My* roof! I ain't nowheres near the jail! I can see all over the neighborhood from here. I can see your house."

I carried the phone to the front window and looked out. Our bedroom is on the second floor so I had a pretty good view of anyplace on Lonnie's roof that he could see my house from.

"I don't know where you are, buddy, but you ain't on the roof. Not yours, anyway."

"Yes, I am! Help me! You gotta help me! Oh, Lord, I'm so sorry! I'm so sorry! I won't never do nothing like this again."

"Nothing like what?" Like that mattered right now. "Never mind. I'll be right over. I'm hanging up, but I'm coming right over. Wherever you are, just hold on, okay?"

"Okay. Hurry!"

I pulled my clothes on while I hopped downstairs, and ran across the street in my house shoes and with my shirt flapping open. I got Lonnie and Leona's spare key out from under the fake-stone turtle by the back door and let myself in.

The smell hit me between the eyes: like cough drops on steroids, and some other stuff underneath.

When I snapped on the kitchen light, there was Lonnie, crouched on the kitchen table, holding onto the edge for dear life with one hand and clutching his smartphone in the other.

"Tiny! What are you doing up on the roof? Go back down and call the fire department!"

I was just glad he'd called me instead of 911.

"I am not on the roof. Neither one of us is on the roof."

He gave a sad little chuckle and shook his head. That made him sway forward and backward, which made him tense up and whimper.

"Here," he said, "take my phone and call the fire department. I don't care if I do get wrote up in the paper."

"I'll get you down," I said.

"Will you, Tiny? I don't want you to fall off, too."

"We ain't neither one of us gonna fall off the roof. I promise you that."

"It's awful steep," he said. "It's awful steep."

"It ain't no steeper than it was that time we put the Santa up there, remember?"

He shuddered. "I remember."

"But we got down, didn't we?"

"Yeah."

"And we didn't break no bones doing it, did we?"

"Naw."

"It's okay, Lon. Close your eyes and I'll lead you down to the kitchen. Okay?"

"Okay. Okay."

He squinched his eyes closed. I took his hand and helped him ease onto a chair, onto the floor, to the back door, and back to the chair, where I sat him down. A lot of that cough drop smell was coming from him, but I kinda had my doubts he'd got into this fix on cough drops.

"Here you are, safe and sound in your kitchen."

Lonnie opened his eyes, shoved his phone into his shirt pocket, and draped himself over the back of the chair like his bones felt all rubbery.

"I lost my nerve," he said. "I thought I was up to it, but I just plain lost my nerve, and that's all there is to it."

"Up to what? Other than no good, that is." I took a couple of deep sniffs. *Grandma Florence?* Yeah, the cedar chest where she kept the quilts we slept under when we visited her. *Furniture polish? Oh, lemon.* Still some stuff I couldn't identify, but smelled familiar. "How'd you do it?"

"I didn't do it. I told you, I lost my nerve."

"I mean how'd you manage to buy something from Scrappy? I was watching you the whole time he was around."

Lonnie couldn't help grinning a little at his own cleverness.

"When the two of you hared off and left me in the shack, I found me something interesting and picked it up. There was prices on it, so I tucked the money into where I took the stuff from."

"What stuff? Lon, you ain't doing dope, are you?"

He glared up at me. "You think I'm crazy?"

I wasn't about to answer that right then, so I just said, "Well, what stuff?"

"I took my phone with me so I could call you from up there, and so I could take pictures to prove I done it."

"You did call me from up there, and how would a picture prove it?"

"Tiny, no offense, but can't you follow a simple English sentence? I wanted to call you from the air, and I wanted to take pictures to prove I was flying."

We were both silent for a minute.

Then I said, "Flying."

Lonnie looked me in the eye, his neck starting to red up. "Yes."

"Flying flying. Not like in a plane or something."

"No."

"Flying. Like Peter Pan."

"Like Don Juan. I told you about him."

We were both silent again.

Then I said, "Huh."

He pointed a trembling finger toward the windowsill over the sink. I went over there and picked up a little bitty screw-top pot and a half-empty bottle. Each one had its top off. Each one had a label pasted on it that said Fly.

I sniffed them; each one was putting out those smells that had hit me when I came in and that reeked off of Lonnie.

"I rubbed that ointment on my arms, see, and then I drank off half of the potion. Next thing I knew, I was flying around the back yard, just like a bird. I landed on the kitchen dormer and I climbed up onto the top of the roof so's I could see your house. I was gonna fly over and go *Boo* in your window, but I lost my nerve. It was a scary feeling; I ain't gonna lie. I don't never want to do that again." He shivered. "Oh, Lord, I might not never get over it."

"Tell you what," I said. "How's about you come over to our house and take a hot shower and sleep in our guest room?"

Lonnie looked up with red-rimmed eyes. "Could I do that? I'm telling you: I'm so weirded out, I don't wanna spend the night here, all by my lonesome."

"Sure, come on. Grab a toothbrush and some clean underwear or whatever."

It took him a while, him having to haul himself up the stairs and ease himself back down. It was near midnight when I tucked him in.

That smell was still bugging me, even though it washed off of Lonnie in the shower. I'd brought the pot and the bottle over with us, and I kept sniffing them and trying to think what it reminded me of besides cough drops, Grandma Florence, and furniture polish. I kept thinking about summer at the river, where we camped out in an RV and fished off the dock and—

I carried Lonnie's magical stuff into my and Mary Lee's bathroom and opened the linen closet. There was a plastic bin on the second-from-the-top shelf where Mary Lee kept sunscreen and Epsom salts and stuff. I pulled it down, and there was a pot just like Lonnie's. The label on the top said Fly.

Now, I know dang good and well Mary Lee never bought a flying ointment in her life, and I know I never flew like a bird, and I remembered, now, rubbing this stuff on my legs and arms and neck.

To keep away the flies and mosquitoes and sand fleas.

I even remembered Mary Lee telling me she bought it at the local Farmers' Market, and that it was made by somebody local.

They don't get much more local than Scrappy.

~*~

Lonnie slept until ten the next morning. He came drag-tailing down to the kitchen clutching his head and belly and looking like The Walking Dead.

Mary Lee's barky little housemutt, Angelface, didn't help him any, I don't think. I told her to hush and gave her a dog treat in some kind of puzzle gizmo that Mary Lee favors. I don't see the point of teasing a poor dumb animal, but Angelface seems to like it okay and it keeps her quiet, which is all I cared about at the moment.

"Good gosh a'mighty," I said to Lonnie, putting a mug of coffee and two aspirins across the table from my place. "Have this quick."

He did, groaning, holding his head and rubbing his gut.

The bottle and pot from his house were in the middle of the table. He pushed them away from himself.

"Oh, Tiny, my head hurts so bad! I never knew magic made your head hurt and your belly sick. Why don't they tell you that? It wasn't in the book. You reckon it's because Leona's a Baptist? Maybe people whose wife ain't a Christian don't get headaches and belly aches."

"That could be," I said. "I wouldn't know. But I do know that people who don't knock back half a pint of vodka on top of two beers and a pizza don't get hangovers as much as the ones who do."

After a couple mugs of coffee, Lonnie quit moaning and said, "What?"

"Whaddya mean, 'What'?"

"What'd you say about vodka?"

I picked up the bottle and sloshed around what liquid was left.

"Vodka," I said. "Plus herbs and stuff." I picked up the pot. "Same thing in here, with something mixed in to make it into a ointment. I called Scrappy this morning. This stuff ain't supposed to *make* you fly; it's to keep *off* flies."

Lonnie glared at the containers between us.

"No," he said. "He's lying to you."

"Mary Lee bought some of the same exact stuff last summer. You used it, then. You're supposed to rub the pasty stuff on you and spray this liquidy stuff on your clothes out of a squirt bottle."

"No."

"You used some last summer, Lon. The only flying I noticed you doing last summer was fly *fishing*."

I was pretty proud of that piece of wordplay, but Lonnie wasn't having it.

"No."

"But—"

"I was up on the roof last night. How do you explain that? Do you see any ladders around the outside of the house? How'd I get onto the roof, if I didn't fly?"

"You were not on the roof. You were on the kitchen table." Lonnie snorted.

There was a scratch at the door. Don't ask me how Homer always knows when Mary Lee is away, but he never scratches to come in unless he knows she isn't there to say no. The other outside dog wouldn't come in the house if you paid him, but Homer is a people person.

I let him in. He sloped his ugly self over and licked Lonnie's knuckles. Lonnie snatched his hand away like Homer had acid for slobber.

"He knows," Lonnie whispered. "He knows I been dealing with The Dark Arts."

"Aw, for—"

"He mighta come over to the side of the angels, but he still knows."

"Lon—"

"Scrappy must have one version of that stuff that he sells to the public, and a magic version that he sells to special customers, there at the junkyard. I ought to tell Leona. He oughtn't to be allowed."

I seriously doubted Leona would give any credence to Lonnie's tale, and I was fairly sure she'd ask for my version before she went leading a mob with torches and pitchforks out to the junkyard. But one of the things a friend does is protect a friend from his own self.

"As I recall," I said, putting some toast in, with no regard whatsoever for the state of Lonnie's stomach, "nobody offered you any. You decided you wanted some unearthly pleasure, and you bought you some under the counter without Scrappy's knowledge or consent. Now, have I got that right or not?"

He shifted in his chair like it was too hot for his skinny butt.

"So," I said, clanking a skillet onto the stove and getting ham and eggs out of the refrigerator, "what, exactly, is it you're going to tell Leona? You gonna tell her you been flying up onto the roof with forbidden warlockerly magic potions? Or you gonna tell her you threw back enough vodka to make a bear dance?"

Lonnie's mouth opened and closed a few times. He stared at Homer like he thought my dog was gonna give him some useful advice, one daring devilish rascal to another.

The butter started bubbling and I slapped a slab of ham into the skillet. When the smell hit his nose, Lonnie turned that pale shade of green Mary Lee wants me to paint the living room.

"I'm going home," he said, and bolted for the door. He paused long enough before he slammed it behind him to say, "Last night didn't happen. Never even happened. Okay, buddy?"

"Whatever you say, Lon."

~*~

"What's Lonnie been up to?" Mary Lee asked me about a week after the wives got back from their thing. We were sitting in the living room with the television running, waiting for Jeopardy to come on.

"Up to?" I stopped reading a live-versus-artificial-bait article in Camp & Forest but I didn't look at Mary Lee.

"Leona says he's been as mild as milk, and he dressed up and went to church with her all three times this week."

"Huh," I said.

"So, while we were gone. . . ."

I turned a page I hadn't read yet and said, "Uh-huh?"

Mary Lee didn't say any more. I stared at the magazine and tried to catch her expression out of the corner of my eye. I couldn't.

"Uh-huh," she said at last. "That's what I thought."

She patted me on the arm and got up. "I'll make us some coffee."

"Decaf," I said.

"I know," she said. "I know."

Lonnie, Me, and the Ugly Dog Contest

Mary Lee rattled the little old weekly paper our town puts out every Wednesday, which meant she'd read something she thought I needed to hear. She was done eating, and was just looking through the paper to pass the time while I chewed.

"What's up?" I buttered a second piece of rye bread to go with my second helping of mashed potatoes and cabbage-and-bacon. A fella my size needs a lot of feeding, and I like to take good care of that.

She folded the paper open to the article she wanted me to see and slid it across the table.

I looked at the page. "20% off tire rotation at Shug's Tire Barn?"

"No." She tapped the paper where she wanted me to read. "This one."

"Well, move your finger. This one?"

"Talk about can't lose!"

The library was holding an Ugly Dog contest a week from Saturday, with the entry fees paying for the trophies and what was left over going to the Children's Summer Reading Program.

"Don't seem fair, though," I said. "Our three would take first, second, and third, and have a three-way tie for Worst In Show."

Mary Lee did that wrinkled-up-nose giggle that makes me feel like a teenager again.

"Angelface isn't ugly," she said, reaching down to rub the ears of her yappy little housemutt. "She's cute-ugly. And Goliath isn't worth the trouble of wrestling him in and out of the car. Besides, you know and I know there's only one sure candidate in this house."

"Homer."

Homer is our middle-sized mutt. I named him Homer because he's ugly as home-made sin, so I couldn't hardly disagree, even if I'd wanted to.

"And what's the prize? A trophy? What's it look like, an ugly dog?"

Mary Lee picked up the folded paper and slapped my arm with it.

"It looks like a trophy. You know — trophy shaped. You know!"

Of course I knew; I was just picking at her for fun, how married people that like each other do.

She said, "Plus, a little package of dog treats and a dollar coupon to the Friends of the Library Used Book Room."

A dollar don't sound like much, but they sell paperbacks at twenty-five cents each. That dollar meant four westerns for me, or two westerns for me and two something elses for Mary Lee, or maybe she'd get five magazines at ten cents apiece.

"Well, that sounds like fun," I said. "Do the dogs have to be clean?"

"I think that would be considerate."

"Considerate for who? Not me, that's for sure."

Mary Lee slugged back the last of her sweet tea and started cleaning up the kitchen.

We both knew the conversation was over, and we both knew how it had ended: Mary Lee would enter Homer and I was going to wash the dog the day of the contest.

~*~

"Seem like he'd be uglier if he was dirty," my best friend, Lonnie, said that evening when I told him about it.

"Mary Lee said to wash him," I said, and even Lon, fool that he is, knew that was that.

"At least he don't mind it," he said. "Not like that first time, eh?"

He jabbed me in the ribs with one of his bony elbows. I'm a big guy — which is why they call me Tiny, of course — but that don't mean a elbow to the ribs don't hurt. It just means people laugh like you're kidding if you say "ouch." So I mostly don't.

"No," I said, "he likes it now."

"That's 'cause he's scrofulous," Lonnie said.

"He's what?"

"Scrofulous. 'Member? Last time we went to visit Father Dan, and he said some of his parishioners was scrofulous? That they went to confession every week when they hadn't done nothing interesting since their last confession?"

"He said they was scrupulous, Lon. That's a whole nother thing."

We were sitting on the rail of Lon and Leona's back porch, eating cherries and watching the lightning bugs come up from the weeds. Lonnie spit his cherry pit out into the yard instead of into the cup his wife, Leona, had given us.

"You get a cherry tree coming up out there, Leona's gonna have your hide."

"No, she won't. She'll be glad to save the money from buying cherries."

He was probably right, at that, but he spit the next pit into the cup.

"Anyways," he said, "Homer is eat up with religion. He just pure loves gettin' dunked."

Lonnie thinks Homer came — really — from hell, and that we saved him and converted him. Once Lonnie gets something fixed in his mind, there's no use arguing with him about it. Lucky for me, not much gets fixed in there, so we get along pretty well, all told.

"I thought Baptists was 'once saved, always saved'," I said. "Besides, me and Mary Lee are Methodists, and Methodists don't dunk. Nothing religious about liking to take a bath."

"Maybe he's a backslider. Maybe it didn't take all the way the first time."

See what I mean about these fixed ideas he gets?

"Whatever," I said.

He whipped out the so-called smartphone he got a while back and started *beeping* and *booping* on it.

We had the porch light off so that we could see the lightning bugs and what stars the glow from town didn't drown out, and the phone screen flared like a television in a dark room.

"That thing's gonna ruin your eyes," I said.

"No, it ain't. It's got some special kinda thingummy that makes it not."

"Uh-huh. What are you doing, anyways?"

"I'm looking at the liberry website to see who-all's entered."

"They got that on the internet?"

"They got dang near eve'thing on the internet, Tiny. Don't you know that?"

"Buddy, if I had a nickle for everything I don't know, I'd be a rich man." And if I had a penny for everything Lonnie don't know but pretends he does, I'd be twice as rich. But that would be mean to say, so I kept it to myself.

Lonnie's hand twitched so hard he almost dropped his phone.

"What is it?"

"Look!" He held the phone up to my nose.

"Don't shine that thing in my eyes! You wanna burn out my corneas or something?"

"Read it!"

"Just tell me. I got the light-blindness, now. Man! So much for star-gazing!"

"I'm sorry, buddy. I'll tell you what it is. Guess who's got a dog in the contest."

"Thought you was gonna tell me."

"Guess first."

"If I guess, I won't need for you to tell me."

He wagged a finger and made a clicking sound out of the side of his mouth that meant he thought I'd said something brilliant.

"Well, I'll tell you, then. A gentleman of our mutual acquaintance named. . . . Guess."

"Lon—"

"Mr. Meriweather Fitzbottom, Esquire."

"Scrappy?"

Scrappy (born Meriweather Fitzbottom) owned one of the town junkyards. Lonnie thought he was a warlock. Lonnie doesn't live nearly as exciting a life as he thinks he does. On the other hand, everybody who hangs around with Lonnie generally leads a way more exciting life than they wish they did, so it evens out.

"He's got the dogs for it," I said. "He might just give Homer some competition. Which dog?"

"Says it's Cujo."

"Which one, though, I wonder." Scrappy had two dogs that I knew of, and they was both named Cujo. For all I knew, every dog he'd ever had was named Cujo.

"Maybe we can find out. See what Homer's chances are."

"What's it matter?"

"He might enter one, and then find an uglier one and bring that one in, instead."

"So what?"

"So that would be cheating."

"This ain't the lottery, Lon. First prize is a plastic trophy, dog treats, and a buck's worth of used books."

"But it wouldn't be honest. You wouldn't want the liberry to get took advantage of, would you?"

"I don't think the library is too worried about that, as long as they raise some money for a good cause." I spit out my last cherry pit and worked my way off the rail onto the porch. "Gonna help me wash him on Saturday morning? Not this Saturday, but the one after?"

"Sure. Sure."

"Okay, then."

I hollered in to tell Leona goodnight and went home, as happy as if I'd had good sense.

~*~

Me and Mary Lee never had kids, which is probably why we ended up with three dogs, but there was a few kids in the neighborhood — kids of friends of ours — who liked to come around. Mary Lee generally kept a bag of cookies or Little Debbies or whatnot in case one of them dropped in or came carrying a message or something.

So, a week after Mary Lee showed me the contest announcement, I got in from work to find Jack and Ella Maclemore's youngest, Blaine, sitting in my place at the table scarfing down Star Crunches like they was M&Ms. I kind of eyeballed him, hoping he'd take the message and move, but he just eyeballed me back.

Mary Lee put a cup of decaf and a plate with a Star Crunch on it next to Blaine and patted the chair for me to sit there.

Blaine wiped his mouth on the back of his hand, in spite of the perfectly good folded up paper towel Mary Lee put next to his plate. "You see the news yet?"

Kid's five and he talks like he's fifty. Comes of being the youngest, with eleven years between him and his next-up brother.

"No," I said. "What's up?"

You never knew, with Blaine. It could be a new Lego toy at the big-box store, or it could be a horse rescue story, or even politics.

"We're in the contest together."

"What contest?"

"The ugly dog contest."

"Now, how is that possible," I said, "when you don't have an ugly dog?"

Truth is, Blaine had a dog so ugly, it looked like a burlap bag full of knuckles. I think it's half toy pitbull and half Gollum with a side of bat. Blaine's mom, Ella, found it dumped outside the warehouse where she's night watchman and brought it home, and Blaine and it latched onto each other. It always made Blaine fighting mad if anybody remarked on her appearance — Lucy the dog, I mean, not Ella — so I was surprised he had entered her.

"You're just being nice," he said, like he was saying *tormentful* in place of *nice*. "Everybody keeps telling me how ugly Lucy is, so I'm entering her in the contest. Maybe I'll get her a trophy and some special treats and get me some free books."

Mary Lee patted Blaine's shoulder and gave me a look, but I didn't know what kind.

After Blaine practically licked his plate and sucked up about half a gallon of milk and left, I asked, "What was that all about?"

Mary Lee shook her head. "He's been waiting for you to get home so he could tell you that."

"You think he wants me to withdraw Homer?"

"No," she said. "I think he wants Lucy to beat Homer."

"Huh," I said, and thought about Lucy a little. "She might, at that."

~*~

When Lonnie got home and I told him, he said, "But Blaine always claims Lucy's about to grow into her beauty. He wouldn't put her in a ugly dog contest."

I said, "You're the one that's always ragging him about how homely she is, getting him all riled up and all."

Lonnie snickered, then had the grace to look ashamed of himself, which he ought to. I'm not saying I never gave the kid a little tease, but I — no, I told myself, I needed to be ashamed, too.

"At least he's facing facts," I said. All the same, there was something kind of sad about a kid admitting his best friend looks like ten mile of bad road.

"I gotta have another look at that dog," Lonnie said. "Just to refresh my memory. Maybe she ain't as homely as I'm thinking."

"Whatever floats your boat," I said.

But, after supper, Lonnie came over with some pie Leona had baked and said, "I went and visited with Jack and Ella and told Blaine how cute Lucy's getting, but he ain't backing out. He's still putting her up for the contest. And I'll tell you the truth; that dog's pretty plain."

"That dog's plain like a octopus has arms," I said. "That dog's so far beyond plain, it can't even look back and see it."

"You think so?"

"I know so. If ugly was brains, that dog would be a rocket scientist. But don't tell Blaine I said so."

Lonnie smacked me on the shoulder four times by way of friendship and left looking happy.

~*~

Saturday came and no Lonnie. I wasn't surprised. We hadn't set a dog-bath schedule, and Lonnie likes to sleep in on Saturday. Besides which, Lonnie avoids Homer whenever possible, since he's never got over believing the poor goofy dog started out life as a hell-hound.

The contestants were supposed to be there at one, so Mary Lee gave me an early lunch and shooed me out the door.

"You'll have time to wash Homer and change into dry clothes," she said. "Don't forget to shut him onto the porch after he's clean."

"I won't." We both remembered the time I'd washed him before her grandmother came to visit, and he turned up to say hello with a fresh coat of dead chipmunk all over his back and a little furry tail tucked behind his ear.

I drug out the big wash tub and ran it half-full of water while Mary Lee filled some gallon jugs from the hot water tap and lined them up on the porch.

Goliath went somewhere and hid, but Homer came and pranced around and stuck his paw into the tub and gave me reproachful looks until I warmed things up with the hot water from the jugs so it suited him. I barely caught him from jumping in and splashing the water all over creation, not to mention me. He knew the drill; he let me pick him up and lower him in. He laid down with just his nose sticking out, then stood up and grinned.

No, unlike any other dog God ever made, getting him in the water wasn't a problem. What I was gonna need Lonnie for was getting the dang dog out before the contest was done and over.

He took turn-about laying down and standing up. It seemed to tickle him, being two different heights. He was high-rumped and long in the shanks, so his belly was barely wet when he stood up, but most of the tall went out of him when he folded those old giraffey legs under him.

Mary Lee let me use some of her Rosemary Botanical shampoo, saying it would bring out the red highlights in his wiry black hair. Red highlights in black hair looked good on Mary Lee, but Homer was gonna look like a campfire just before Smokey Bear shows you exactly what he thinks of campfires.

After I had him washed and rinsed, I snuck the hose over the edge of the tub and let the cold run into it. He gave me some heart-breaking looks and whined, but I was on the clock, so I waited until he was standing up and wrestled him out. The dog is only the size of a beagle — not counting those stilts he uses for legs — but it's pure muscle and, cold or not, every muscle he had wanted to stay in the water. You wouldn't think a dog could get you in a half-Nelson with his neck, but he pretty nearly did before I got him onto the patio. Mary Lee had put a stack of old beach towels out there for me to dry Homer off with, but I was pretty much beyond anything a towel could do for me.

Homer was still damp when we lured him into the car. We put an old blanket in the back seat and over the floor back there. Mary Lee yucked and complained about the wet dog smell, and I silently gave myself points for not mentioning that washing him had been her idea.

We agreed it would be better to leave him in the car while we checked in for the contest, which was set up in the municipal parking lot next to the library. They had it blocked off with yellow CAUTION tape, had a check-in desk for contestants (or contestant owners, I guess I mean), and had folding chairs set up for the judges and the spectators.

I hadn't thought to ask who was going to judge the contest, but now I could see for myself: Miss Imogene, who was the town librarian for about a hundred and fifty years but still looked about sixty; Conrad Bakersfield, whose family had owned the pet shop for four generations; and Brenda Ann Mudder, last year's County Fair Queen.

Scrappy was already lurking back behind the building where the Friends of the Library sold used books, one of his Cujos on a chain. Blaine and his mom were back there, too, Blaine holding something that looked like a lump of clay all swelled up with bee stings that was probably Lucy. I could see a plaid flannel elbow sticking out from behind the building and a red high heel, so I guessed that meant at least two other contestants.

"You're the last one," the young fella who checked me off his list said. "I thought we'd have more than five entrants."

"Nobody much wants to admit their dog is ugly," I said, "let alone prize-winning ugly. Next time, ask people to donate if their dog *ain't* ugly, and you might get more play."

Mary Lee jiggled my elbow to pay Homer's entrance fee. It was ten dollars and I put down a twenty, and Mary Lee said, "Keep the change."

I said, "I intend to," and she laughed and drug me away.

From across the lot come a familiar "Oo-oo!" Leona waved at us and followed Lonnie's bee-line over to us. Mary Lee and Leona started chatting away, just like they didn't live next door to each other and run tame in each other's houses.

Lonnie rubber-necked around, hunting for my dog. "How's Homer? He still in the running?"

"Good to see you, too," I said. "And thank you so much for helping wash him, like you said you was gonna."

"So he's here?"

I should know better than to try to be sarcastic with Lonnie. You never can tell when he's going to get it and when it's going to whizz right past him without making a dent.

"He's in the back seat, resting up from his bath."

Lonnie said, "There's only five contestants."

"I heard," I said. "Me and Blaine and Scrappy and who else?"

"Louisa Pennington's Mugsy and Paul Lanscap's Beauregard."

"Aw, those dogs ain't ugly! At least, no uglier than they're supposed to be." Mugsy was a big bulldog and

Beauregard was a Basset hound. Like I told Lonnie: neither one was a beauty queen, but they looked pretty good for the kind of dogs they were born as.

It's funny. I didn't really care about the contest, but all of a sudden, I did. Why I wanted three independent witnesses to give me a certificate saying I had the ugliest dog in town, I couldn't tell you, but I just got all on fire with wanting Homer to win.

"You been checking out the competition," I said to Lonnie. "What do you think Homer's chances are?"

"I went out and had a nice long jaw with Scrappy yesterday," he said. "I looked all the Cujos over and talked up the bad points of the leastest ugliest of them, hoping he'd bring that one, but he brought the ugliest one, after all."

"Which one is the ugliest one?" They both looked pretty much the same to me, all fangs and slobber.

"That one thats head is so big its hindquarters pops up every time it barks."

"Good choice! What about Lucy? How's Lucy looking?"

Lonnie chuckled. "Blaine give Lucy a bath, too, and scrubbed her with coconut oil and shea butter and jojobob and I don't know what all. That dog's so shiny, you could take her up a hill and send light-flashy messages with her. Made her fur so fluffy, you can see her scalp all over."

"Whoo! It don't look good for Homer, buddy."

"Good thing it don't matter," Lonnie said, cutting me a look that said he meant it to be a dig.

He had a point, but it kind of irked me, so I just shrugged.

Miss Imogene stood up, her being Mistress of Ceremonies as well as one of the judges, and said they'd be calling the contestants in order of when they'd checked in this afternoon. She announced the prizes — second was dog treats and a dollar coupon on used books without a trophy, and third was just dog treats.

Louisa brought Mugsy out and everybody applauded politely. You could tell Louisa had only brought him to show him off, and that she thought he was cute as one of those kittens Mary Lee coos over on the internet.

The next one they called was Blaine. He carried Lucy out. Miss Imogene asked him to put her down so the judges could get a good look at her, but he said she was scared. He carried her over to them and held her out and turned her around so they could evaluate her from every angle. I could see her shivering, and how her tail was tucked in under her belly. Blaine looked like he was about to cry, and I decided right then that I'd withdraw Homer. Just wouldn't take him up when they called me. If the kid wanted the win that bad, I reckoned a grown-up could let him have it.

Blaine went and stood next to Louisa, with Lucy's face tucked into his armpit.

Beauregard the Basset hound pulled Paul out and snuffled over to blow snot all over the judges' shoes. He was in good Basset hound form today, with his jowls almost dragging the ground and his bloodshot eyes bagging down and his big floppy feet tripping over his own droopy ears.

"Meriweather Fitzbottom," Miss Imogene called, and Scrappy lumbered into view with Big-Headed Cujo on a length of chain that coulda held Frankenstein.

Cujo snarled, Scrappy said, "Silent, Cujo," and the dog snapped his jaws together so hard I could hear his teeth meet. The hairs on Cujo's spine stuck up like dinosaur scales on that kind of dinosaur that has scales sticking up on its spine.

The judges all reared back in their chairs while they contemplated Cujo. When Scrappy took him to stand in line with the other contestants, the other dogs all ootched over away from him and gave him that wall-eyed look where they tried to keep him in view without making actual eye contact.

Miss Imogene called my name. I shook my head and opened my mouth to say I withdrew, but the car door opened and shut behind me and Mary Lee shoved the business end of Homer's leash into my hand.

"No," Lonnie whispered. Then he said, "No, Tiny! You ain't gonna show that dog!"

Mary Lee said, "That is the idea," and nudged me forward with a handful of fingernails to my back.

I led Homer forward through a wave of laughter from the crowd.

When I got a look at my dog, I could see why.

Leaving a damp dog in the car to dry might not be the best idea. His hair was fine on one side — apart from its natural medium-long, wiry, red-shot bristliness, that is. The other side swirled and poked out in all directions, like somebody had glued a boxful of cowlicks all over him. One of his pricked-up ears had got turned inside out. I turned it back the normal way, but he shook his head and there it went inside out again.

Conrad and Brenda Ann, the judges who weren't Miss Imogene, kinda squinted at Homer, like he hurt their eyes. Miss Imogene's eyes were wide, wide open, though, and she was going, real soft, "Hoooo, hoooo." I thought she was doing a owl imitation. Then her eyes begun to water and I realized she was doing her damnedest not to laugh.

"He don't usually look this bad," I said, not wanting to ruin Blaine's chance to win. "He just slept funny."

Miss Imogene took a deep breath and said, "Please join the other contestants." That woman was a lady, clear down to her toes.

The judges didn't consult long.

"Third place winner: Beauregard!"

Paul came up to the table, waving to his cheering section, and bowed to each of the judges as he scooped up Beau's bag of treats.

"Second place winner: Cujo!"

Scrappy gave the rest of us a dirty look — I guess, because one of us was going to take first place — and went to get his treats and coupon.

"And the first place trophy goes to. . . ." Miss Imogene paused for effect. Blaine and I locked gazes. We both knew Mugsy wasn't in the running. "First place winner is Homer!"

Mary Lee and Leona whooped.

I felt sick at heart. I couldn't hardly stand to look at Blaine when he heard, but I did.

He grinned all over his face. He pulled that thing he called a dog up and kissed her right between the eyes. He walked over to me and raised his chin and said, "Ha! I *told* you my dog wasn't ugly!"

Paul gave Blaine Beauregard's treats, saying they weren't the kind he liked. Scrappy gave Blaine his book coupon, saying he only ever read ebooks. And I gave him Homer's trophy.

~*~

"What's the matter with you?" I asked Lonnie while I was grilling for our celebration cookout and he was watching me do it. "You had your face on wrong all afternoon. Anybody'd think you didn't want Homer to win."

"Truth be told, buddy, I didn't."

"Why? He ain't *your* dog. What do you care if the whole town thinks he's a tourist attraction? It's no skin off your nose."

Lonnie plinked a fingernail against his lemonade glass — no beer for us, with Leona there.

"Lon," I said. "Why do you care if Homer won?"

If that sounds like an accusation dressed up like a question, that's because it was.

When he still didn't answer, I whispered, "Lon, you wasn't holding book on the contest, were you?" Meaning, was he taking bets like a horse race bookie.

He was honestly shocked. "No! No, of course not!" He checked to make sure Leona hadn't heard. "Don't even joke about it. No, I never would. Gambling is one thing I'm with Leona on. Gambling's wrong."

"That's 'cause you always lose."

He drained his lemonade.

"Lon," I said, "how much did you lose? Tell ol' Tiny."

"I did not gamble on the ugly dog contest."

"Uh-huh."

"But I might have . . . I might have had a little . . . challenge kinda thingie going on with Bert Lamb."

"Your barber?"

"A month's worth of haircuts against a dozen raspberry-filled donuts from that snooty pastry place up on Concord Avenue."

"And you lost?"

He sighed like he staked the family fortune on one roll of the dice. "Yeah, I did."

"You bet against Homer?"

"Yeah, I did."

"You bet against Homer being the ugliest dog in town?"

"The ugliest dog in the contest, yeah."

I flipped the burgers over.

"You," I said. "You bet a dozen raspberry donuts that Homer wasn't as ugly as Lucy or Cujo. Any of the Cujos."

"Yeah."

I couldn't say it, because I was kinda choked up, but it's things like that that's why Lonnie is my best friend.

Lonnie, Me, and the Resurrection Eggs

"Come on over, Tiny," Lonnie yelled from across the street.

I beep-locked my car, made that call me sign with my other hand, and went on in the house. I just got off a long shift at the plant and I wanted a beer and a shower, not a long ramble through the wilderness that passed for my best friend's mind.

The phone rang before I kicked my shoes off. I went on and answered it; not even Lonnie would believe I wasn't home, when he'd just seen me walk in.

"Come on over, Tiny," he said again. "I been waitin' supper."

I've known Lonnie most of my life, and there was something in his voice that told me he had a surprise up his sleeve. That's hardly ever a good thing.

"Lemme take a quick shower and change into my home clothes. Fifteen minutes."

"Okay. Did Mary Lee leave you any more of that potato salad?"

"I'll bring it."

"And the You-Know-What."

Lonnie's wife, Leona, had dragged my Mary Lee off on a church meditation retreat. I hoped Mary Lee wasn't going to come home a hardshell Baptist like Leona, who was a fine person but sometimes a little too particular about what was okay and what wasn't. How she got to be married to Lonnie was something I'd always been a little afraid to ask.

Anyway, Lonnie and me had been batching it for the three days they were gone, pitching in the food our wives had left us and watching action movies on Lonnie's big screen TV. I'd been careful to only take over a third of Mary Lee's potato salad every night, because Lonnie loved it as much as everybody did, and I knew anything I left in his refrigerator would be gone the next time I wanted some.

After I cleaned up and got into my jeans and baggy shirt, I grabbed the night's share of potato salad and the You-Know-What — beer — and went on over to Lonnie's, around to the kitchen door.

"Finally! Rip me off one of them cold ones, would you, buddy?" He opened the refrigerator, hip-bumped it wide open, and pulled out a heavy glass plate. "Ta-daaaaa!"

The plate was one of those cut-glass dealies the ladies use for parties and pitch-ins, with oval indentations pressed into it to hold two dozen or so hard-boiled egg halves. It was full.

"I made Resurrection Eggs! Leona always makes them for picnics, and they're so good with ham and potato salad, and she didn't make any, and I got a taste for them. How 'bout that?"

I was impressed. I'd never known Lonnie to make anything in the kitchen except a mess, but these looked like the real deal.

One of the real deals. Every woman made them a little bit different. Mary Lee made hers with mayonnaise and onion powder and mustard and salt and pepper and paprika. She called hers Stuffed Eggs. Leona mashed her yellows up with sweet pickle relish and Miracle Whip and called hers Resurrection Eggs. Lonnie's had so much pickle relish in them you couldn't hardly see the yellow.

"I will not eat green eggs and ham," I said and laughed.

Lonnie *planked* the plate on the table. "It wouldn't kill you to try them."

Served me right for quoting literature to Lonnie.

I picked one up and bit into it. It tasted like nothing on Earth, and I don't mean that in a good way. It was hard to tell, with all the flavors whupping the tar out of each other, but I would take an oath in court there was some kind of fish in there. Sardines? Anchovies?

Lonnie popped one in, managed to chew it up and swallow it, and looked at me all sorrowful and betrayed, like *I* had made the damn things.

I apologized to my stomach and swallowed my bite whole. For a few seconds, I thought Lonnie's Resurrection Eggs were going to live up to their name and rise again.

"Lonnie," I said, "what have you done?"

"Well. . . . Leona's are good, and Mary Lee's are good, so I figured if I put in everything they both use and my own special touch, mine would be better."

His own special touch. Yeah, that would be sardines. "I can't honestly say they are, buddy."

"But we gotta eat 'em. I made a whole dozen."

"Why, Lon? We watching Cool Hand Luke tonight?"

"No. Why?"

I didn't even answer that. I'd just show him the movie, and he'd see.

"We gotta eat 'em," Lonnie repeated. "I can't waste all them eggs. Maybe the girls would like them?"

He actually had a point. Our wives ate a lot of stuff Lonnie and me wouldn't unless the wives were watching. But I couldn't stand by while a couple of loving, trusting women touched these things to their tastebuds.

"Tell you what," I said. "I'll buy 'em from you and give 'em to Homer." Homer was my dog, also known as The Living Garbage Disposal.

"I don't know. Giving good food to a dog. . . ."

Good food wasn't in question, but Lonnie was getting that cross-eyed contrary look, and I had to think fast.

I leaned across the table, like I was telling a secret and somebody might hear. "Lonnie, do you know what you made here?" I tapped the plate. "These here are what the recipe books call Deviled Eggs."

His jaw dropped. "I made Deviled Eggs? In Leona's kitchen?"

"I'm sorry, buddy, but yeah, you did."

"Homer would eat 'em. He'd like 'em."

Homer would like a dead skunk, but never mind.

"Let's just leave these be for right now," I said, "and eat the ham and potato salad. I'll take these home. You buy some more eggs tomorrow and Leona never has to know."

Lonnie reached out a hand and we shook on it.

"Tiny, you're the best friend I got in the world."

"And you're my best friend, Lonnie." Kinda sad, but it was true.

Lonnie, Me, and the Block Party Cookoff

The wives came back from the Neighborhood Association meeting all pumped up about something. Lonnie and me, who'd been doing yard work at Lonnie and Leona's while they were gone, gave each other a look. When the wives got all het up about something, it usually meant a Project. Not a project, a Project.

My wife, Mary Lee, said, "Oh, Tiny, you boys are going to love this!"

"Yes, ma'am," I said, saluting her.

She slapped my arm a little, gave me that *oh, you rascal* grin that still kills me after twenty years, and said, "We're having a block party!"

Leona said, "More than a block, though."

Mary Lee nodded. "More than a block. These three blocks, from Anderson's Hardware on over to the park, mostly."

Lonnie loves block parties, and he'd been agitating for years for Leona to talk the Neighborhood Association into throwing one. So you'd think he'd be high-fiving the rest of us and doing his chicken dance, but no. He'd got himself stung by a ground wasp while he was picking up downed branches and was miffed because I'd been telling him right along to put on gloves and he wouldn't, so he was in a contrary mood.

"What for? That would have been great, back earlier, but it's too dang hot, now. And what's to keep it from pouring down rain?"

Leona, who is either a saint or missed her calling as a kindergarten teacher, said, "The ten-day forecast says it's supposed to be cooler and partly cloudy next week, and next week is when we're doing it. Ace is getting us the permits."

"That's pretty soon," I said.

Lonnie muttered, "Is that so, Captain Obvious?" We all ignored him.

Mary Lee said, "We're raising money to help send Clint, that oldest Maclemore boy, to New York City with the high school band. They thought they had it covered, but then Jack Maclemore got laid off, and Clint wouldn't have any spending money or anything to eat on. He's just a third trumpet, so it doesn't matter to the playing of the band, but it would break his heart if he didn't go."

The Maclemores lived on me and Mary Lee's side of the street, and it was our house the Maclemore kids spent half their time at, but it was Lonnie they pestered the worst. Sometimes he wanted to tease them until they screamed, sometimes he wanted to play along with whatever game they were running through the neighborhood, and sometimes he channeled a crabby old man and chased them off his lawn.

Lonnie said, "I'd give a hunnert dollars if he'd take that li'l peanut, Blaine, with him, and another hunnert if he'd leave him there." He'd never got over Blaine's losing the library's Ugly Dog contest when Lonnie'd bet a box of raspberry donuts that Blaine's Lucy was the flat-dab ugliest dog in town.

"Now, Lonnie," his wife said.

Mary Lee said, "We're going to rent a couple of those bouncy house things."

When Lonnie's eyes lit up, Leona said, firmly, "For the kids."

Mary Lee said, "But the main thing is a BBQ rib cook-off. That's where the money comes in."

Lonnie perked up again. I love to grill, don't get me wrong, but I never saw anybody who loved a grill more than Lonnie. He'd wanted to build a brick one on the slab where his shed used to be before he accidentally blew it up, but he decided to buy a portable one instead. He loved it like most men love a car.

"We have to pay to grill or something?" He would have, too.

"No," Mary Lee said. "It's a cook-off." And she explained how we'd have grills all along the street, kind of blocked off so the kids wouldn't run up and burn themselves, and jars in front of each grill. Folks could sample a short rib for quarter. Then they'd put a dollar in the jar of the rib they liked the best. If they wanted a whole meal, they'd pay five dollars at the side-dish booth and get corn and green beans and bread and six long ribs from their favorite griller. "The hardware store is sponsoring it," she said. "The cook who raises the most money gets a $25 gift certificate to Anderson's Hardware."

It sounded like a good deal to me.

Lonnie winced like his wasp sting had throbbed, and groused, "Why don't the hardware store just give Clint the money and leave us all out of it?"

The wives protested with stuff like, "What fun is that?"

The real reason, of course, is that giving Clint the money wouldn't bring a crowd of people into the neighborhood, where they'd see the hardware store's name plastered all over three blocks and maybe stop in for those mousetraps they'd been meaning to buy.

"Sounds like a lotta work." Lonnie raised up his hand and stared at it so the wives could see where he got stung.

"Oh, honey!" Leona started clucking over him. "Why didn't you say something as soon as we came in?"

"Didn't want to make a fuss," he lied.

She ripped open a cigarette from the pack she kept in the medicine drawer for just such an emergency, wetted down the tobacco, and tied a wad of it on Lon's sting with about half a mile of gauze. Neither Lonnie nor Leona ever smoked, and that pack in the medicine drawer was probably ten years old if it was a day. Mary Lee keeps one, too.

Leona patted Lonnie's poor old mummified hand and said, "Fortunately, this block is blessed with plenty of big, strong men and energetic women."

"You boys run along to our house," Mary Lee said. "Leona and I need to make a shopping list."

Mary Lee is a good woman, but a little of Lonnie goes a long way with her. If it wasn't for Leona, she'd have no patience at all with him.

Lonnie was glad to go, since his wife was a hardshell Baptist and didn't hold with drinking, and I always had a few brews in the fridge.

By the time Mary Lee came home and sent him back across the street to Leona, you'd have thought the whole block party was his idea.

~*~

The hardware store bought napkins and plates, industrial-sized cans of corn and green beans, and soda and bottled water. The locker plant gave them a discount on the ribs. Restaurants gave us some carry-out boxes and plasticware-and-napkin packages. The wives made desserts — well, mostly the wives: I made my world-famous peach and pineapple dump cake.

And, sure enough, the weather that day was perfect: overcast and mild, with no breeze to blow the smoke into people's eyes.

By the time we pulled back the sawhorses and let folks in, I was about worn out. All us "big, strong men and energetic women" had started at the crack of dawn, setting up the side-dish booth and the grill barriers and about a million card tables and folding chairs for people to sit at and eat. The rent-a-bounce guys had staked their bouncy houses down on a couple of lawns, so any kids who fell out would fall on the grass and not the street where we could get sued.

Everybody had put their dogs in the house or in their back yards, and between the *yips* and the *woofs*, the *whoops* of the kids in the bouncy houses, the grillers trying to get folks to come to their grills to try their ribs, and people talking over all of it, it sounded like a carnival without the merry-go-round music.

Lonnie was in his element, fussing with his coals like he was the guy who invented fire.

Like I said, Lon's good on the grill, but I wouldn't be trying any of his ribs today.

"Some folks like it hot," he'd said, "and I'm just the boy to give it to 'em. I've been experimenting with this new hot sauce, and it'll take the top of your head right clean off."

"I'm kind of attached to the top of my head," I'd said. "It keeps my brains from getting the inside of my hat all gummy."

He had a sign on the barrier in front of his grill that said, WARNING! HOT! HOT! HOT! EAT AT YOUR OWN RISK!

The neighborhood kids hung on the barriers when they weren't bouncing, especially around Lonnie.

Just as I hustled past with a fresh stack of divided Styrofoam plates for the side-dish booth, I heard Blaine Maclemore say, "What happened to your hand?"

Yes, Lonnie's hand was still wrapped up. When it had stopped hurting, it had started itching, and guess who just has to scratch an itch, even if it aggravates it?

Lonnie said, "Me and Tiny was digging for treasure in my back yard, and this big ol' dragon up and burnt it. Leona hadda spit tobacco juice on the burn to cool it down."

Blaine shouted, "Liar! Liar! Pants on fire!"

"Yeah? Well, you just go dig back there where them tree branches is cleared away and see if it don't happen to you."

"Truth to tell," I said, scared the goofy kid would go do it, "that big ol' dragon looked an awful lot like a nest of ground wasps to me."

"It was enchanted," Lonnie said, which took me aback, *enchanted* not being a word you would ever imagine coming out of that particular source.

Blaine shouted to the crowd, "Look out! Mr. Carter is a pants-on-fire!"

Lonnie shouted, "That's 'cause I wiped some of this here barbeque sauce off on 'em! Yessiree, this is some hot sauce!"

I wouldn't have believed it, but Lonnie's grill had the longest line in front of it all day, and any given table always had at least one person with sweat pouring down a red face.

None of the grillers were eating anything but ice cream their spouses slipped them, it being too hot behind the grills, and the sight and smell of all that meat for hours on end being too much of a good thing.

Finally, though, the crowd thinned out as the sun got low. The grillers turned off the gas or put the lid on the fire bowls so the coals would burn out.

The bouncy houses came down, and the leftover sides — not much left over, really — got packed away and divided up between anybody who wanted any.

The cooks and the rest of us, who were frazzled with picking up trash, toting supplies and pots of hot side dishes, and keeping children out of mischief, sat down to eat. We would put everything away before dark, but right now we needed a break.

My favorite — because you just know a man called Tiny spent the day sampling the ribs — was Jack Maclemore's, with his secret apricot-rosemary glaze, and I had a double order of those in front of me.

Lonnie had a plate of his own. His eyes were bugged out and he was sweating so hard it was dripping off the ends of his hair.

I guess everybody was so tired, we each left somebody else to look after the kids. You know what that means: Nobody was.

When things got quiet, I kind of halfway noticed it, but I just figured we all got too tired to talk all at the same time, like happens sometimes. I guess I thought the kids had gone in to watch television or play video games. The dogs had pretty much quieted down, once the strangers were out of the neighborhood. Only Mary Lee's yappy little house dog, Angelface, was still rubbing her snot all over the front window and keeping the world safe through her superpower of never shutting up once she got started.

But then all the youngsters were at their parents' sides or clustered around our table, staring at Lonnie and smothering giggles.

He did look pretty funny, like a googley-eyed flamingo with the sunburn, and I grinned, too.

Then — as Lon said that time he blew up his shed — *BLAMMY!*

The lid to Lon's grill flew off, mercifully missing anybody, hit the asphalt at an angle, slid all the way across to me and Mary Lee's side of the street, hit the curb, and flipped end over end, finally tipping real gentle to cover our lawn sprinkler. Even Angelface shut up and watched.

Lonnie looked at it. He looked at the rib in his hand. He looked at his grill.

He said, "Good thing that didn't happen while all that crowd was here. I better dial that sauce back a little."

It didn't take long for the kids, who were as scared as they were impressed by what had happened, to finger Blaine Maclemore as the genius behind it. He'd turned up an old, forgotten Super Cherry Bomb in his parents' garage, and the kids had closed it into Lonnie's grill while nobody was paying attention. They'd expected a *boom*, but not a *blammy*. I imagine there was a wide array of discipline going on all up and down the block.

Lonnie said, "If that'd been you or me, our daddies would have tanned our bottoms. We wouldn't of been able to sit down for a week. Somebody ought to take a hickory switch to that little skunk."

"Now, Lonnie," Leona said, "he's only a child."

"That's what worries me."

Me, I was just glad he'd found a Super Cherry Bomb and not, say, a stick of dynamite. One shed-sized explosion was enough for any neighborhood.

Marian Allen

Lonnie, Me, and
the Reptiles of Tybee Island

Mary Lee came in waving a piece of paper, and kissed me before she even closed the door or put down her keys or took off her coat or anything.

I kissed her and gave her a big old bear hug, and hurried to close the door. "It must be a thousand degrees below out there. You trying to do global warming on our dime?"

"I'm sorry," she said, shucking her coat, "but this is so exciting. Oh, Tiny, wait 'til you hear!"

What it was was some kind of a Friends of the Library convention in Savannah, Georgia. Any member of our local Friends group who volunteered to go would get to stay free in a cottage on Tybee Island, just off the coast.

"Leona and I volunteered! And we can bring our husbands!"

She showed me the dates, and I allowed as how I could get that week off work, and she kissed me again. This was a win-win situation, if ever there was one.

We had Lonnie and Leona over for supper, and he acted like he didn't much like the idea, but we all knew that was just Lonnie being Lonnie.

"I never left nothing in Georgia; why would I want to go to Georgia?"

Leona just said, "Because I'm going, and you can't stand your own cooking."

I couldn't stand his cooking, either, so I saw her point.

Mary Lee's sister said she'd come over to feed and water

our dogs and Lonnie's cousin's oldest girl said she'd housesit for them and take care of their cat.

So off we went.

It would have been a completely uneventful drive if Lonnie hadn't zigged when he should have zagged and took us east and south instead of south and east. You ain't lived until you've gone through the Cumberland Gap by moonlight. The wives loved it, and Lonnie acted like he'd done it on purpose, but his knuckles were so white they were like little extra headlights.

But we got there and found the cottage, which was really pretty and not far from the beach.

Next day, the wives hit the convention and Lonnie and me went exploring. The town started a block to our left, and what looked like wilderness started to our right, so Lonnie just naturally wanted to go right.

He flexed his scrawny, ropey muscles and said, "Let's go wrestle some alligators."

"I don't think they have alligators in Georgia, Lon."

"Then let's wrestle whatever they got!"

He pulled out that little smartphone he's so in love with and started snapping pictures of sand and palm trees and me.

"Smile, Tiny!"

"Smile, your own self." There's probably more pictures of me on Facebook than there are of the President, and I'm not even *on* the damn thing.

The "wilderness" was only a couple hundred feet, and then we were on the beach, and I'll tell you what: it was worth the trip. Even Lonnie stopped jabbering for whole minutes at a time while we walked and gawked, just about alone, it being December.

Before too long, we got to where the town came right down to a plaza and a pier. We followed the street inland, past a couple of restaurants, a bunch of gift shops, and a tattoo parlor, and ended up circling around to our cottage, where we ate and took naps until the wives came in and dragged us out for dinner.

Everybody who knew Tybee Island and heard we were going said we had to eat at The Crab Shack, so that's where we went.

~*~

"Look, Tiny! Alligators! I told you there's alligators in Georgia! Told ya so! Told ya so!"

Outside the restaurant, they had this big cage with pools and plants and stuff, with signs all over it like, "Feed the alligators!" and "Live alligators!" I trailed Lonnie like a barge following a tug, knowing without being told that he was circling the cage hoping to find a way in.

He said, "Betcha I could wrestle me one o' them bad boys."

I snorted. "How 'bout that one? The one the size of a Cadillac El Dorado?"

"I seen 'em doin' it on YouTube. You just gotta know how."

"And do you know how? No, you don't."

We were on the opposite side of the cage from the wives when Leona gave a big squeal.

Lonnie was past me like a tall, skinny streak of light, his shout of, "I'm comin', honey," disappearing into the distance almost before I saw him going. Mary Lee was over there, too, so I was right on his heels, scared to death that one of the gators was out and after them.

I felt about half relieved, half mad, and all foolish when Lonnie and me rounded the gator pen and found the wives cooing and clucking over a bunch of damn cats. They'd spotted a mini high-rise with Cat Shack painted on it. There must have been seven cats in it or peeking around corners near it. Whoever put it there wasn't any kind of a fool: right next to it was a door with a GIFT SHOP sign.

I was so hungry I could have eaten one of those alligators, but the wives just couldn't wait to shop, so we followed them in, me kissing some dollars goodbye in my mind. Leona carried most of the cash in their family, so I don't know what Lonnie was thinking, assuming he ever does.

While the wives were yakking with the gal behind the counter, Lonnie and me went through a narrow door and down a step into another room. It was lined with tall cages full of birds. I mean big birds. Not, you know, big like Big Bird, but a damn sight bigger than sparrows.

Turns out parrots and cockatoos and like that live a long time, and these ones had outlived the people who owned them, and the Crab Shack people rescued them instead of letting them get put down. I barely read the sign about them biting in time to keep Lonnie from poking his fingers through the mesh.

He went around to every cage, saying, "Polly want a cracker?", and complaining that none of them talked when they just looked disgusted and bored.

We were about to go out and tell the wives to come see when one of them — one of the birds, I mean, not one of the wives — spread out his wings and ruffled up his feathers, and said, "Headlock! He takes him to the mat! What a wrestler!"

I could hear my heartbeat over the laughter of the wives in the other room.

Lonnie moved closer to the bird. "What did you say? Wrestler?"

"What a bout! He struggles up!" The bird groaned. "Scissor hold! Headlock! He's down again. Where's the ref?" The bird made a *ding* sound that I could have sworn was a timer bell. It was pretty amazing.

Lonnie breathed, "It's a Sign."

The wives poked their heads in, scouting around for us, and saw the birds. *Oo*ing and *aah*ing, they came in and Lonnie led me out.

"Lookee here," he said to the counter lady, "do fellas ever wrestle them alligators?"

Her eyes widened and she caught her breath. "I'll have to get my manager." She went into another room and closed the door.

A couple of minutes later, a man almost as big as I am came out. The counter lady hung back inside the doorway, a hand over her mouth.

"Which one of you heroes wants to wrestle an alligator?"

Lonnie flexed his ropey arms and said, "That'd be me."

"You sure?"

Lonnie looked less sure by the second, but he said, "I had a Sign. I know how to beat him. You can have folks make bets, if you want to."

"Lonnie," I said, "I don't hardly think Leona is gonna approve of this exercise, especially if you take bets." Leona is a hardshell Baptist, and doesn't hold with gambling. Or stupidity, come to that, but she'd probably come to be pretty used to that by now.

"No bets," the man said. "This has got to be absolutely secret. We could get in all kinds of trouble if word got out."

Lonnie tipped him a wink, or maybe his nerve was going and it was a twitch.

"Come on," the man said. "We got one out back of here. We keep him away from the others because he's always trying to fight with 'em. We been looking for somebody to take him down a notch. Looks like you're our man. Say, you ain't that crocodile guy from television, are you?"

"That guy's already dead," I said, without thinking, and Lonnie gave me a hurt look.

The man led us outside and to a shed. He unlocked it, threw open the door, and flipped on the light. He kind of crowded us in and closed the door.

"He's over there in that corner," he said.

The alligator was penned in a box that was not much bigger than he was. I felt kind of sorry for him, but the walls of the box were just barely taller than him, so I didn't see how he could not get out if he wanted to. Maybe alligator legs don't lift them up very high or something.

"Go get him, Tiger!" the man said. Whether he was calling Lonnie "Tiger," or whether Tiger was the alligator's name, I don't know.

Lonnie didn't move. Neither did the alligator. We all just stood there. Time stretched out.

Finally, I said, "Is he even alive?"

The man said, "No." He stepped back outside, holding the door open for us. "It's December. All the alligators are hibernating. The ones in the pond now are just fake ones, like this guy." He snapped off the light, closed the door after us, and locked it.

I cut my eyes at Lonnie. He looked like Mr. Mad and Mr. Relieved were having a party and fighting over the tab.

He muttered, "That was a dirty trick."

I said, "Maybe so, but I wish now I'd had money on you. I believe you could have taken a fake alligator, two falls out of three."

~*~

The next morning, Lonnie waved at the wives until they were out of sight, then said those four words everybody who knows him has come to dread:

"I got a idea."

"Oh?" That was always the safest thing to say. Sometimes his notions blew over on their own.

"Let's get tattoos."

"Do what?" I'd known Lon since we were both knee-high to grasshoppers, and this was a new one.

"Tattoos. We passed a tattoo parlor, and that bald guy that was sitting outside with the tattoos all over his arms and neck give me a nod yesterday. I never even really thought about getting a tattoo before, but now I am."

This was bad. For some reason, Mary Lee and Leona count on me to keep Lonnie out of trouble, in spite of the fact that Lon could get into trouble chained alone in the basement of Alcatraz prison.

"Leona don't hold with tattoos," I said. "She says it's desecrating God's holy temple of the body. You heard her say that many a time."

"What Leona don't know won't hurt me."

Leona probably knew more than Lonnie thought she knew. I just figure she decided a long time ago that the only way their marriage was going to work was for her to overlook a damn sight more than other women with other husbands would have to. Sometimes I suspected that Mary Lee felt the same way about me.

"Now how is Leona not going to know you got a tattoo?" You notice we'd already gone from "Let's" to "you." He knew damn well there wasn't a way in the world I'd let some guy poke holes in me and rub ink into 'em.

"I'll get it some place she don't look."

I wasn't about to ask where on his body a man's wife did and didn't look, especially when I knew the man and his wife, and ate with them sometimes. Besides, I could see by the way his eyes were shifting that he was considering and rejecting locations.

"Maybe a tattoo ain't such a good idea, Lon. Maybe you should think it over for a day or two."

He got that muley look that told me he'd dig in harder if I tried to talk him out of it.

"But," I said, "I guess there's no time like the present. You just gotta come up with a spot for it."

His stubbornness flickered to uncertainty again. Maybe all wasn't lost.

I said, "The only place I can think of for sure is between your toes. Even your doctor never looks there." Just the thought of a tattoo needle in between my toes made my feet twitch, but Lonnie's imagination doesn't work that way.

"Say, that's right! That's what I'll do. Gonna get me a little bitty sea turtle right in between my toes." Turns out Tybee Island is known for sea turtles coming there to lay their eggs. Apparently, it's some kind of a big deal, and there was sea turtle souvenir stuff all over the island.

Lonnie swaggered down the street like an outlaw, an impression that kind of suffered when he said, "Should I ought to get a cartoony one or a real-looking one?"

"Whatever you think, Lon. Maybe they show you pictures to pick from or something."

Turns out, they do. It was almost lunchtime before Lonnie finished browsing and trading small talk with the artists and customers and other hangers-around. There was some good-natured teasing of big ol' Tiny, who didn't even want to look at the designs, but nobody tried to talk me into anything, so I didn't mind the jokes.

Finally, Lonnie made his choice (a cartoon — surprise!) and sat down. He pulled off his shoe and sock.

This was my last chance to put the kibosh on the project. "Will it hurt?"

The artist — Watson, he called himself — put on latex gloves.

"Nah," he said. "Just a little bee sting."

He swabbed Lonnie's foot down with alcohol or some kind of cleaner and disinfectant. He braced the toes apart so he could get to that little web of skin right where the toes come together.

I was watching that procedure, so it wasn't until Lonnie said, "*Urp*," that I found out what he would look like as a Martian. Green skin, buggy eyes, skinny body, everything but the bulging brain.

"Here it comes, buddy," I said. "Couple thousand bee stings and you're done."

Watson turned on the electric needle and bent over the "canvas."

Lonnie's eyes rolled up in his head and he slumped sideways in the chair.

Watson turned off the machine.

"You stopping?" Seemed to me, unconscious was the only way to get a tattoo.

"Customer has to be wide awake, sober, and old enough to know better. Two out of three don't count."

Lonnie stirred and opened his eyes. "Is it over?"

"The man says you gotta be awake."

"Uh …. Uh, I'm just hungry, is all."

"Yeah," I said. "Low blood sugar. Let's go grab a sandwich and come back later."

Watson retrieved his toe brace and stripped off his gloves. Being a good businessman, he gave Lonnie a manly handclasp as we left and growled, "Any time, bro."

We talked about anything but tattoos over lunch. Then, pressing my luck, I said, "If you're feeling better, let's go get that job done before the wives come back for the day."

"Nah," Lonnie said, "I'm out of the notion, now. The mood's done passed."

"Whatever you say, Lon."

"Don't feel bad, Tiny. You wouldn't get disappointed like this if you was adventurous, like me. You gotta quit living your life through me, buddy. Spread your wings! Fly!"

I saved his empty coffee mug from being knocked off the table by his flapping arms.

"Turtles don't fly," I said, "and I reckon I'm more turtle than bird."

He punched me in the bicep and gave me a sympathetic smile.

"I guess that's why we get along so good," he said. "Opposites attract."

That probably made me a genius, but I didn't say that out loud.

Lonnie, Me, and
the Ugliest Couch in the World

"There's no accounting for taste, Lon," I said.

"Well, I know, but *look* at it," he said.

"I'm not looking at it twice," I said. "That's above and beyond. I told you I'd help you move it, but you never said nothing about looking at it."

"I hear ya, Tiny," he said. "I think I owe you a couple extra slices of pizza for that."

Lonnie's wife, Leona, had gone and bought a couch and told them her husband would pick it up. Lonnie approved of saving eighty bucks on delivery and borrowed the truck from work.

Now, when you're the biggest guy around, like I am, you just naturally expect that any moving that gets done, you're going to be part of the crew. So here I was next to him on the loading dock, waiting for the guy to bring papers for Lonnie to sign, trying to keep from looking at Leona's new couch.

"Know how many couches this makes that we've had," Lonnie said, as if I cared, "including sofas, divans, davenports, and loveseats? Ten. Over time, you know, counting ones folks give us when we couldn't afford to buy any."

The man came back with the papers and Lonnie signed them.

"Wait a minute," he said, holding the man back from his work. "Before you go in: Is this the ugliest couch you ever seen or not?"

Lonnie, Me, and the Ugliest Couch in the World

It was stuffed so thick on the arms they looked like upholstered balloons, and the rest was so thin it was practically a bench with a towel over it. The pattern looked to me like pink and green chickens, but the man said it was peonies. But, he admitted, kinda squashed-up, draggle-tailed peonies.

We lashed the couch into the truck bed and got in.

"Whaddya think?" Lonnie was driving, and it wasn't like him to ask for directions, but this was more by way of advice. "Should we go on the freeway where more people will see it, or on the surface roads, where they'll have to see it longer?"

"Freeway, so we can get this thing indoors quicker."

Unfortunately, Leona and my wife, Mary Lee, had each given us "honey-do" lists, so we had some stops to make.

At the gas station, Lonnie got out to pump and I heard him hollering at somebody. I scrooched around to see if I knew who it was, but it was a guy in a van with out-of-state plates on it.

Lonnie bawled, "I want you to come over here and look at something. I ask you, is this the ugliest couch you ever seen, or what?"

The guy whistled and said, "If that was my couch, I'd shoot it in the head and bury it after dark."

"I thank ya, sir, that's all I wanted to know."

When he got back in, I told him I was disappointed in him, subjecting an unsuspecting visitor to that couch, and it wasn't showing our state in a very good light, but Lonnie didn't care.

At the hardware store, Lon drug the whole staff out and made them vote. They voted yes, it was the ugliest couch in the world.

One of the clerks said, "Dang! It looks like somebody ate it and it didn't agree with 'em."

When we got home, we carried the monstrosity in and asked Leona where she wanted it.

She gave a ladylike little shriek and grabbed the phone.

Seems this was not the couch she was looking for.

After about half an hour on the phone with the furniture store manager, crying and shouting and calling on God to witness and threatening brimstone and lawyers, Leona hung up and said we had to take the thing back and get the one she had really ordered.

I don't know about Lonnie, but I was flat-out bushed by the time we swapped couch number ten for couch number eleven, which wasn't much to write home about, but looked like perfection itself after the other one.

Lonnie ordered two pizzas and I silently dared Leona to forbid either one of us to crack a couple beers out in the back yard. She mished her lips together, but she didn't say a thing about it.

We could hear the wives in the kitchen, laughing themselves breathless, but all we felt like doing was eating and drinking and enjoying the breeze out on the porch.

After Mary Lee and me got home, she kept breaking into giggles, so I finally asked her, "What's so funny?"

"You know," she said. "That horrible couch Leona said Lonnie got."

"*She* ordered it," I said.

"She never did!"

"Well, she did and she didn't. I mean, she didn't, but he thought she did."

Mary Lee shook her head at me. "Now, why in the world would Leona order a couch like that?"

"Why in the world would she marry Lonnie?"

I had her there.

"Oh, well," she said, "I guess there's no accounting for taste."

Marian Allen

Lonnie, Me, and the Loaded Lady

Lonnie and me had just finally finished setting up his and Leona's Christmas tree when she got back from Wednesday prayer meeting and play practice. My wife, Mary Lee, had wanted to come help, but I told her we couldn't cuss right with women around, so she stayed home and wrapped presents.

Leona, a hardshell Baptist, went to church every time they unlocked the doors, and she always volunteered to direct the Christmas pageant, which practiced right after Wednesday prayer meeting so the hound of heaven could at least lick at the heels of the kids in the play, so Wednesday looked like a good choice for this particular project.

Lonnie Carter is my best friend in the world, but he's a certifiable fool. That's just something you got to accept about Lon and then go on from there.

For instance: Him and Leona always have a real tree instead of an artificial one, so driving out to Leona's cousin's in the country to cut one is a yearly adventure. Lucky for me, it's kind of a personal thing with them, or Mary Lee and me would get drug into it, and Lonnie in the woods with an ax is an experience I am absolutely not wanting to have.

But my point is, they don't have a big ol' box full of plastic branches to store the tree stand in, so we searched the attic for an hour before we went downstairs to guzzle one of the beers I brought with me, and Lonnie found the stand on a top shelf in the walk-in pantry where he'd seen it every day of the world.

Anyway, we wrestled the tree up with only a few minor scratches and bruises each and even got it pretty straight by the time Leona came in.

She flopped onto the couch without even taking off her coat. She looked so frazzled, I nearly offered her a beer before I remembered who I was talking to.

"Rough day at the pageant?" Lonnie leaned his tall, skinny self over to kiss her on the forehead without breathing beer on her, and barely caught himself from somersaulting into her lap.

"The children are so sweet," Leona said, not really answering the question, to my mind.

"You draft some locals?" That's what Lonnie called the non-churched friends of the church kids who the church kids got to come be in the pageant. It was part of Heart of Jesus' Junior Missionary program. I hated to tell Leona, but bribery, blackmail, and threats of violence got as many young locals through the door as Christian witness. She probably would have said something about fighting fire with fire or using the Devil's own tools against him, but it would have hurt her to hear it, no matter what she said out loud, so I kept what I knew to myself.

"There are five children from the neighborhood in the pageant," she said.

"The Herdmans?" Lonnie said it every year, and got a chuckle out of it every time. Out of himself, that is, not out of anybody else.

The Herdmans were the family of wild kids who took over the play in that book, The Best Christmas Pageant Ever.

"No," Leona said, in that tone women get when they say *no* to the same question for the fifty-millionth time. "John Beckman is back; he's been to church on his own several times; we have hopes of him joining us in fellowship one of these days. He brought his little cousin, Batey."

Lonnie scrubbed at a patch of pine sap on the back of his hand, wincing when it pulled at his hairs. "What kind of a name is Batey?"

"Short for Bateman."

"Bateman Beckman? What kind of folks does that poor child have?"

"Well, that's the thing. His father's passed and his mother's in jail for shoplifting, so he's staying with John's folks until she gets out."

"You better watch your purse."

I should have gone home, right then, but I knew Mary Lee would want a report on Leona's pageant, so I stayed.

"That's not fair," she said. "Just because his mother stole, doesn't mean the child is a thief. Does it, Tiny?"

Tiny is me. I played football in high school, where the coach always said I was a defensive line all by myself, so naturally everybody calls me Tiny.

I said, "Sometimes it doesn't, sometimes it does. Mary Lee always watches her purse everywhere anyway." If she didn't switch purses to go with her outfits, you'd think it was a baby, the way she keeps track of it. In fact, no matter which one she's carrying, I always call it Wilson, just to mess with her.

"Well, tonight," Leona said, "Batey came up to me and tugged at my sleeve and said, 'There's a lady outside and I think she's loaded.'"

Lonnie said, "How old is this squirt?"

"Four, I think."

"Does he know what *loaded* means?"

"I didn't ask. Right about then, parents started coming to pick their children up. I told a couple of the men, and they had a look around and didn't find anybody, so we just left. I need to call Pastor Billy and tell him about it." She finally looked at what we'd spent the evening working at. "Doesn't that tree look a little wockerjawed to you?

Lonnie, Me, and the Loaded Lady

~*~

The next Wednesday, Lonnie and me went with Leona. Mary Lee had been pushing it all week, worried for her best friend and the pageant kids, and she had got me worried, too. I was so worried, I even brought my dog, Homer.

Lonnie didn't like it, of course. "You can't bring that hell hound to church!"

"Why not, I'd like to know? He's housebroken."

"Because he's a hell hound! He'll prob'ly bust into flames!"

"Lon, this dog is probably a better Christian than you and me put together. He'll be fine. If we run into any trouble, you'll be glad he's there."

Leona objected, too. "If there is a drunken woman coming around, I don't want you to scare her to death."

Lonnie said, "What *do* you want us to do? Chase her off?"

Leona looked uncomfortable. "That doesn't seem very Christian, does it? I want you to…. Oh, I don't know! Ask her what she wants? Help her?"

I took Homer, anyway. Maybe not the best idea I ever had, but I hate to give it to Lonnie. Of course, if Lonnie hadn't been Lonnie, it wouldn't have been as bad an idea as it was.

~*~

Lonnie and me got interested in watching Leona work with the kids and forgot to patrol. He was watching because he's just pure nuts about his wife, like I am about Mary Lee, and I was watching because I could see now how she managed life with Lonnie. The technique looked pretty similar.

Anyway, Leona was working with the shepherds, wise men, and central characters, so the heavenly host was kind of at loose ends. Most of them were petting Homer and making over him, which he ate up with a spoon. Truth be told, he's a fairly ugly dog, but the kids didn't seem to notice or care.

One little kid grabbed ahold of my finger and said, "That loaded lady is back."

"Heads up, Lon," I said. "Target spotted."

"What? A spotted what?"

"This little kid says he saw You Know Who."

"Elvis?" He finally caught up. "Oh!" He squatted down beside the little boy. "Where, honey? Where is the lady?"

The boy went mute, probably freaked out by two big men and an ugly dog all staring at him. "Outside," he whispered. "Outside."

Outside was a big place.

I extracted Homer from his fan base, and Lonnie and me took him into the hall. The glass double-doors at the end of the hall were locked, of course, for security, but Leona had given me the key, so I let us out and locked up behind us. Right away, I felt like we maybe should have called the cops. It was late November, and cold and black as Dick's hatband, as my grandpa used to say, although the grounds were lit up with security lights.

"He's prob'ly just making it up to get attention," Lonnie said. "His father dead and his mother in the slammer and all. He prob'ly just wants people to pay attention to him."

"Have you been watching daytime television again?" Lonnie worked first shift, but he'd got some kind of machine he could program to record shows without commercials, and I'd walked in on him watching People's Court a couple of times, and that bald-headed guy who's on practically every show on TV. Steve Harvey. "You been watching Steve Harvey?"

"I know a little psychology. I read this article on Facebook that talked about it."

We rounded the corner of the church building and almost plowed into her.

She was tall and meaty, built good but kind of on the overgenerous side, which I like, but which I don't exactly tell Mary Lee, her being sensitive about her own wonderful well-builtedness. This woman had dark hair that didn't shine in the artificial light, so, according to what I hear from Mary Lee, that meant it was probably a bad dye job. She just had a flimsy coat on, and a dress and the kind of shoes you wear when you have to stand up for a long time.

"Hey, there," Lonnie said. "Can we help you?"

"No," the woman said, in a hollow kind of voice. "Can't anybody help me."

Lonnie surprised me by saying, "The Lord can help you, Sister. Come on into church, where my wife is. She can lead you to the Lord." Mary Lee had read me from a magazine about how husbands and wives can start to be more like each other, but this proved it so hard I thought I might have to write to the magazine and tell them about it.

"All I want to be led to is Matt Brenner."

"Matt Brenner? Little bald-headed squirt, wears bow ties?"

That's when we found out that Batey both did and did not know what *loaded* means.

The woman pushed back her coat and pulled out a revolver.

"Gun!" Lonnie yelled loud enough to wake up the folks in the church graveyard. "Woman with a gun! Run for your life!"

"You sexist pig," the woman said, and pointed her gun right at Lonnie.

Homer pulled his leash out of my hand and jumped her.

She was solid enough not to go down, but the gun fired into the dirt.

Lonnie took his own advice and bolted for the church. I probably would have followed him, but Homer, bouncing back and forth between the woman and me, had got his leash wrapped around my legs.

"Damn it, Homer!" I bent down to get free, and the next bullet went over my head.

Around the corner, Lonnie was pounding at the glass doors, yelling, "Woman with a gun! Let me in! Let me in!" He stopped pounding and apparently took off running again, his voice getting smaller as he went, yelling, "Help! Help! Help! Help! Help!"

I got Homer loose and he jumped the woman again. The gun went off, chipping the corner off a church brick. She pointed the gun at Homer.

Everything went red behind my eyes. "Don't you shoot my dog! Don't you do it!" I knotted up a fist and showed it to her. I've never laid a violent hand on a woman and on damn few men, and she sure could have killed me, but I don't think she coulda put enough bullets in me to keep me from paying her back if she hurt my dog.

When the red passed, I saw Homer standing at her feet, ruff raised, growling like a grizzly bear, and her with her hands raised and her finger off the gun's trigger.

"I'm not shooting your dog," she said. She bent down to put the gun on the ground. Homer stopped growling and licked her on the chin.

She knelt beside him and hugged him till he squeaked, his tail wagging like somebody was feeding him.

Lonnie's voice got louder, and he came around the far corner of the building in a full circle. "Help! Help! Help! Help!" He skidded to a halt on the blacktop. "Oh."

"Yeah. Oh."

"Good work," he said. "I distracted her, and you overpowered her when she wasn't paying attention."

"Uh-huh."

She looked up at Lonnie like he had some kind of answer for her and said, "Can I talk to your wife?"

~*~

Leona said it was a scandal in the church. She said Matt Brenner — that little bald-headed squirt in the bow ties — had kept the loaded lady as a mistress for years until he got caught at it and the preacher made him give her up. Apparently, she didn't want to be given up, and she'd come gunning for Matt.

Leona passed her on to the pastor, who passed her on to the pastor of a church on the other side of town.

Heart of Jesus hired a couple of rent-a-cops to handle security. That was fine with me. Church is just too damn dangerous for a man and his dog.

Lonnie, Me, and the Blowed Up Santa

"You're gonna put a *what* out for Christmas?" I thought I heard right, but my ears was covered up with cap flaps, so I couldn't be sure. My best friend, Lonnie, was helping me string Christmas lights along my gutters, which meant he was standing on the ground passing the lights up to me and I was on the ladder doing the work.

"A BLOWED UP SANTA!" His cheeks got all red from shouting so loud, and faces appeared in windows all up and down the block.

"Okay, all right," I said, patting at the air to tell him to lower the volume. "That's what I thought you said, but it didn't sound likely. Is Leona gonna stand for that?"

Leona is Lonnie's wife, and she doesn't hold much with Pagan trappings to a holy day, and she puts Santa Claus into the Pagan category. My wife, Mary Lee, carries on a friendly dispute with her over it, pointing out that Santa Claus is slang for Saint Nicholas. But Leona's a hardshell Baptist, and Catholic might as well be Pastafarian as far as she's concerned.

"Leona loves it," Lonnie said. "I showed her a picture of it, and she almost cried, she loved it so much."

"Really?"

"Yep."

"A Santa?"

"Yep."

"Well, okay." I came down, moved the ladder along, and went back up.

Lonnie, Me, and the Blowed Up Santa

Mary Lee and I love decorating for Christmas. We love everything about Christmas, period. If we ever manage to have kids — and we ain't quit hoping — that kid'll be so Christmassed out, it'll be dizzy clear through Easter.

Lonnie and Leona's kids, though, if they ever have any, won't know if they're coming or going. What with all Leona's rules and all Lonnie's breaking of 'em, their kids'll be as like as not to grow up with double personality disorder or what have you.

Mary Lee says Lonnie won't ever have kids, because everybody knows a jackass can't reproduce. Lonnie's one of those friends your wife doesn't know why you have. Her and me and Lonnie and Leona all grew up together, though, and you couldn't split us with an atom.

"Tiny? Hey, Tiny?" Lonnie shook the ladder to get my attention. It got my attention, all right; I nearly went off into the hydrangeas. And, when a man my size hits the hydrangeas, they get hit and stay hit.

"Cut it out, Lon! Just say my name, don't kill me!"

"Sorry, buddy, but you gonna help me put that Santa up?"

"Sure, I will. Course, I will."

Lonnie wasn't much for climbing onto ladders, but he always helped me set out the solar-powered candy cane sidewalk liner glowsticks and the wire frame reindeers with the twinkly lights all over 'em and the flashy-light wreath on the front door. I didn't figure it was too much for him to ask me to help him pump up one little inflatable Santa for his lawn.

~*~

"Where in the world did you *get* this thing?"

I toed the pile of red vinyl that took up way too much of Lonnie and Leona's front yard.

"I ordered it out of a magazine. It come yesterday."

"Like this? I mean, wasn't it in a box or something?"

"Yeah, it was in a box."

"All folded up nice and neat?"

"Yeah."

"And you unfolded it and slopped it all over the yard like this because why?"

"You been in our house. You think we got room for this bad boy in the house? We're gonna put it outside, so I unpacked it outside."

That kinda made sense, so I said, "We don't have to blow it up with our own personal air, do we? Did it come with a pump?"

"Come with a pump and a connector hose and all."

"Where's that?"

"Still in the house in its box."

"And the pump and hose are still in the house in the box because. . . ."

"We got room in the house for that."

"How about you bring it out here," I said, promising myself an extra bourbon ball for not raising my voice, "and we'll get to pumping."

"Wouldn't it be better to put it where it goes before we pump it up?"

I tried not to sound surprised when I said, "That's good thinking, Lon. You know whereabouts Leona wants it?"

He looked at me like I asked him what he fed it or something.

"On the roof," he said.

"On the roof?"

"Well, sure. So's it'll show up good."

"And Leona wants it on the roof?"

"Yeah."

"She wants it on the roof?"

"Yes!"

I was saved from asking him again by Leona, herself, coming out onto the porch all bundled up against the cold.

"Lonnie says you want this Santa Claus on the roof," I said, trying not to sound like I was tattle-telling.

"I do," she said, and hugged herself. She bounced up and down on her toes a few times and, just like Lon had said, she got kinda teary-eyed. "Wait 'til you see it!"

Well, that must be some Santa, is all I could think.

"So," I said to Lonnie, "how we gonna get this up there?"

"I got that all figgered out." He held up a hand like *waaaait for it*, leaned around the porch railing, and pulled out a nylon rope. "Ta-daaaa!"

I looked from the rope to the folds of red stuff stiffening in the cold.

Lonnie patted me on the shoulder. "It's all right, buddy. You ain't had time to study on it like I done. I got it all figgered out. Look." He took one end of the rope and climbed into the Santa stuff.

"Now, watch out, Honey," Leona said. "You don't want to get footprints all over it."

"I'll wash it off if I do," he said, fumbling around, turning over stacks of deflated inflatable. "Look, Tiny. Now, look. Looka here. Right . . . right here."

He finally found the piece he was hunting for, looped the rope around and snapped it in a chokehold, and handed me the other end.

"There you go," he said. "Now you just climb up the ladder onto the top of the roof and haul 'er on up there."

"I do what?"

"Climb up the ladder." He stopped. His brain must have caught up with his mouth and, give him credit, it didn't sound right, even to him. "*We'll* climb up the ladder onto the top of the roof and *we'll* haul him up."

"You first," I said.

I told Mary Lee later that I truly thought his having to go first would kill the idea, and he'd settle for leaving the thing on the ground. But I had miscalculated how deep into pig-headed territory Lonnie had gone. Turns out, he was flat-dab determined, and nothing but Leona could have possibly stopped that runaway freight train, but Leona was all for it.

"Okay, come on," he said. "Let's get this done while we still got some light."

It was light enough, even though the clear skies meant it was as cold as a brass monkey.

Lonnie took the rope from me and paid it out while he ooched up the ladder, not looking down as he went. His and Leona's roof wasn't as steep as some, but I thought Lonnie was gonna go onto his belly before he got to the ridgeline. He threw a leg over the crown so he was sitting astride it.

"Whoo! Man, what a view! Come on up, Tiny!" His voice was about an octave higher than normal, and his Adam's apple was bobbing so hard I could see it from the ground.

Just by way of a friendly kind of meanness, I said, "You got the anchors up there already?"

And he said, "What anchors?"

I laughed, but then Leona said, "Anchors?"

I explained it to her. "You can't just put something on the roof. You got to anchor it down somehow. Old Man Beams showed Lonnie and me all about it last Halloween, when he put that big Jack-o-lantern on his roof."

Leona came out onto the lawn with me and hollered up, "Lonnie, Honey, did you get some anchors? Like Mr. Beams showed you last Halloween?"

Leona and me looked up at Lonnie, and then looked at each other.

I said, "I'll go get some rope and a couple of cement blocks."

"Thank you, Tiny," she said.

As I crossed the street, I could hear her telling Lonnie what I had just told her, and Lonnie claiming he didn't need any anchors. He was talking in that jokey tone of voice he uses when he knows he's saying something stupid that's going to get overruled anyway so he can say it as much as he feels like.

Mary Lee came out to the garage when she saw me rummaging around.

"What does he need that he didn't even think about?"

"Something to hold the dang thing on the roof."

"Maybe he could haul a sleeping bag up there and lay across its feet for the rest of December."

"Be nice," I said.

She saw I was dragging out cement blocks, and brought the wheelbarrow around for me to put them into. She went back into the house.

When I got back to Lonnie's, she had come out the front door and was standing with Leona, looking up at Lonnie and gossiping kinda half-hearted about some woman they both knew.

Lonnie was just sitting up there, holding the end of his rope like a kid with a busted balloon.

"Whaddya waiting for," I yelled, "Christmas? Haul the dang thing up!"

"I need he'p! He's too heavy for me"

"Get hauling! Me and the wives'll feed 'im up."

Mary Lee said, "We will?"

Her and Leona giggled and came over to help me wrestle with all that cold vinyl.

Lonnie gave a couple of pulls, and the piece he had the rope around raised up out of the pile.

"Oh, my Lord," I said, "he's hanging Santa Claus!"

I would have gone with the feet, myself, but Lonnie had snapped that rope around Santa's neck, and up the ladder it went, flopping hat, flat beard, squinched-up face and all. I hoped none of the neighborhood kids were watching; it would give them the heebie-jeebie nightmares, for sure.

With Lonnie tugging, me easing up the ladder with one arm wrapped around unidentifiable Santa parts, and the wives unfolding vinyl and feeding it along, we got the old boy up and draped across the roof-beam.

I showed Lonnie the anchor eyes on Santa's toes and heels.

I said, "I'll go bring four of the blocks up and we'll tie his feet to 'em and start blowing him up. There'll probably be more anchor eyes higher up on him." Then I said, knowing what the answer was before I asked it, "You did bring the blower pump up here while I was getting the blocks outta my garage, right?"

Lonnie looked down the slope of the roof and lost all his color.

I felt ashamed of myself and said, "Does Leona know where it is?"

"Yeah," he said, nodding like one of those bobbly headed dolls. "She knows exactly where it is!"

I hoped he wasn't just saying that. When I got down to ground level, it turned out he was right. She went in, I hefted eight cement blocks, one by one, onto the roof, Mary Lee passed me the ropes, and Lonnie picked up Santa's head and waggled it around, asking me if I'd been a good boy this year.

Leona came back out, lugging a green and yellow blower and yards of electric cord.

"Plug?" I said.

"Back," she puffed.

I sent Mary Lee home for another couple of lengths of rope so I could tie the blower to Santa's cement blocks so the dang thing wouldn't fall off the roof. I felt pretty safe, myself, but the longer this nonsense went on, the less confidence I had of Lonnie living through it. I didn't really think I'd push my best friend off the roof, but I wasn't for certain-sure Mary Lee wouldn't go up after him.

By the time we got — and I use the word "we" loosely — everything set up and plugged in and turned on, the sun was going down. One gold ray broke through a cloud and lit up the front of the Santa as he filled out with pumped air and stood to attention. It hit this ball he was holding. The ball shivered as it inflated, sending silver glitter swirling all around the inside of it and making the swaddled Baby Jesus in there bounce around like a peanut in a tornado.

Down on the ground, Leona broke into applause.

Mary Lee said, "Oh, my God!"

Leona hugged her and said, "I know! I know!" She blew her nose.

I held onto one of the guy ropes with both hands and did not look at Mary Lee.

"She likes it," Lonnie said, proudly.

"Good job, buddy," I said. "You made that woman's Christmas."

"I did, didn't I? Yep. I guess I sure did. And now watch. She don't know about this, yet."

He reached up and goosed Santa in the butt. Apparently, what he really did was flip a battery switch, because Santa lit up all glowy inside, and the Baby Jesus' glitter sparkled. I had a sudden — probably blasphemous — vision of Him ascending into heaven saying, "Beam me up, Scotty."

Down below, Leona squealed, "Oh, Lonnie! I'm gonna call the Praise Chain right now!"

~*~

She must've done it, too, because not an hour went by before cars started snailing along the street, stopping in front of Lonnie and Leona's house — or mine and Mary Lee's, depending on which direction they were going.

The next night, more people came by. Folks in the neighborhood went back to the attic and brought out more decorations and put them up, since it looked like our street was turning into one of those Christmas Village kind of deals.

You're probably wondering what the dogs thought about all this. At first, Angelface, Mary Lee's little house mutt, barked every time a strange car stopped outside the house, but she got over that by the third night of heavy traffic. Goliath, the big outside mutt, never pays any notice of anything or anybody unless they touch our property. One toe on the lawn, though, and he lets out a *woof* that you feel in your back teeth. Naturally, Homer, the middle-size, mostly outside mutt, had to have his nose into everything. If he wasn't trying to eat the plastic candy canes, he was whizzing on the electric choirboys. Good thing those were indoor/ outdoor lights, made to stand up to rain and snow and, apparently, dog water.

Every night, more and more cars crawled down the block and more and more lights and inflatables went up. Mary Lee hung blankets over our bedroom windows, just so we could sleep without having our eyeballs twinkled out by all the lights.

~*~

"Tiny," Lonnie said while we settled down to watch us some Sunday afternoon football, "that blowed-up Santa is the best thing I ever done. Leona's as happy as a clam."

"Where'd you get the dang thing, anyway? Nobody else's got one anything like it."

"Got it out of a internet catalog," he said. "I run across it on my little ol' smartphone, and I showed it to Leona, and she loved it and I bought it." He gave it kind of a uncertain glance out through our picture window and said, "I never expected it to be so big, though."

"I don't know," I said. "Maybe I'm just getting used to him, but he don't look quite as big as he did when we put him up. Course, we're not sitting in the shade of his belt buckle, now."

"That do make a difference."

~*~

But the next day, it was obvious that Santa had lost some of his oomph. He hardly had enough stuffing left in him to hold up the Baby Jesus.

"He just needs some more air pumped back into him," I said. "I reckon that's why the pump comes with him. If you only had to pump him up once, you could rent a pump, am I right?"

"Makes sense," Lonnie said. "Well, let's go do 'er."

"Whaddya mean, 'let's'? Flippin' a switch ain't a two-man job." I was just joking, though. I knew how he hated high places, and I knew how he hated to admit it. "Come on," I said.

I set the ladder on the back of the house this time and sent Lonnie up ahead of me. He was tall enough to stretch out with his toes in the rain gutter and reach up and hit the blower's *on* button. I stood on the ladder and told him when Santa looked all plumped up. Then I made sure he got his feet back on the rungs, with my hand knotted up in his shirt to steady him, and we eased down.

We had no sooner reached the ground when Leona busted out of the back door.

"Lonnie, you'll never guess what! That was The Local Beat on the phone just now. You know, the television people! They heard about our giant Jesus Santa and they want to come do a story about it." She patted me on the arm like she was apologizing to me for their decoration being so special and said, "They want to take pictures of the whole neighborhood. They're doing stories every Friday of Advent about streets with specially pretty lights and all, and they heard about ours and want it to be one of them."

She gave Lonnie a big hug and pinched his cheek.

Lonnie pulled one of her curls and said, "When they coming? Tonight?"

"They didn't know. They're filming a bunch of them and then putting them together all jumbledy, just anyway their editor thinks it would look nice. They might come take the pictures any night, but they'll let us know when they're going to show us."

"I better go home and plug in the lawn," I said, and did.

~*~

The grapevine spread the news all up and down the street. By the next evening, there were so many elves and Santas and giant caroler mice with scarfs around their necks and electric icicles and such it looked like a Christmas Factory Outlet.

I apologized to Mary Lee. "I'm sorry our place looks kinda Scroogey, but I can't see spending the money."

"I'm glad to hear it," she said. I wasn't really surprised; we see eye to eye on most things. She said, "It's not my life's ambition to see our house on the news."

"On the news? They can probably see this street from outer space."

It was right about then the phone rang.

"Tiny? That dang Santa's sagging again."

"He must have a leak."

"What am I gonna do?"

"Go on back up there and give him another shot of air. I showed you how. You did it fine."

"Come on over and hold the ladder for me. Leona don't have the upper arm strength."

"Homer'll be glad to do it," I said.

"Oh, ha ha."

Lonnie wasn't all that crazy about Homer, although Homer acted like Lonnie was his favorite uncle or something. I was telling the truth: Homer would've been glad to hold the ladder. Homer probably would've climbed up onto the roof with him, if Lonnie'd asked him to.

I sure wished I could've sent him over in my place. I really didn't want to go out in the cold, but you do things you don't much want to do, when it's for a friend. So I asked Mary Lee to keep the cocoa warm until I got back.

~*~

It got to where ol' Santa needed to be gassed up every third day, then every other day, then every evening before the Christmas light cruisers came by. And the television people still hadn't come to take their pictures.

The good news was that Lonnie got used to going up the ladder and turning on the blower, so I didn't need to play nursery maid for him.

"If I'd 'a' knowed he was gonna take so much tending to," Lonnie told me, "I would have just showed Leona the picture and let it go at that."

Even Leona begun to have a kind of haunted look in her eyes, like having St. Nick on her roof was only maybe one step better than having a monkey on her back.

Finally, the last Tuesday before Christmas, Leona called. I answered, and she was so excited she didn't even ask to talk to Mary Lee, but just blurted out the news.

"They're coming! The television people! They're coming tonight!"

"For sure?"

"For sure! They called and told me they saved the best for last, and for everybody to turn their stuff on and they'd be around."

"When? After dark?"

"Well, sure, after dark. It wouldn't show up very pretty unless it was after dark."

"They gonna come early and interview you and Lonnie?"

"They didn't say. Do you think. . . ." She must have decided this called for the attention of the supervisor. "Can you put Mary Lee on?"

From Mary Lee's half of the conversation, I gathered that Leona was asking about if she should have refreshments for the television people, and how many Mary Lee thought there would be, and if it would be stingy to have refreshments for just them or if she ought to have an open house, and how much stuff it would take to do it right.

I left them to it and went to plug in and turn on what raggedy decorations we had and check that all the bulbs were working. While I was at it, I made sure Goliath and Homer were in the back yard. I made sure I closed and locked the gate. With people who didn't know the neighborhood driving through gawking at the pretty shinies instead of watching where they were going, that just seemed like a good idea.

Across the street, Leona's Santa looked kinda saggified. But I heard a *whooooooooof* and watched him straighten up and bounce the baby Jesus around like a hot potato.

When I went back in, Mary Lee was slapping together chicken salad sandwiches like she was getting paid for it.

No, no, whoa, time out! "Hey! I thought that was for my lunch tomorrow!"

"This is an emergency. Leona's worried about having enough food for her open house, so I told her I'd bring these over. If they don't eat 'em, we can bring 'em back."

"If the television people don't eat 'em, Lonnie will. You know how he is about your chicken salad. He likes it almost as much as I do."

"Aw, aren't you the sweetest thing!" She stopped working and stretched up and smooched me.

Women. I never knew what was going to make Mary Lee go all honey-darlin'.

She said, "I'll leave a couple here for your lunch. There just won't be any extra for you to sneak spoonfuls of when you think I'm not looking."

And here I'd thought I was putting that one over on her. I should have known better.

By and by, it took both of us to carry the supplies we were contributing to the cause across to Lonnie and Leona's back door. As we walked across, I thought Santa was already drooping some.

I told Lonnie about it when we got in.

"Doggone that thing! Why'd he have to spring a big ol' leak tonight, of all nights?"

"Why don't you patch it?"

"Don't have time."

That, and patching it would mean working on it up on the roof, and that wasn't something Lonnie was likely to favor.

He pulled on his coat and stomped to the back door.

Just as Leona said, "Don't let Rocky out," their twenty-pound Maine Coon Cat shouldered Lonnie aside and made his escape.

Leona gave a little scream and called, "Rocky! Here, baby!"

"He won't stay out long," Lonnie said. "Rattle the treat bag."

He shut the door and we heard his boots on the ladder, then the *clump-clump* of him kneeling and flopping onto the roof, then the *whooof* of the blower.

The phone rang.

The person on the other end of the line gabbled loud enough for Mary Lee and me to hear the noise of it but not the words. Leona faced us and bounced up and down and flapped the hand that wasn't holding the phone. She said, "Okay! Thanks!" and hung up.

"They're here!" Like we couldn't have guessed. "They're down at the far corner!"

She opened the back door and yelled up the ladder, "Honey? They're down at the far corner!"

Lonnie's voice floated down: "I'm a-pumpin' 'im up as hard as I can pump. Here we go!"

Another kind of *woof* came from the back yard, and a catty *yowp*.

"Rocky! Rocky! Here, baby!" Leona cast an accusing look at me.

"I locked the dogs up before I left home. Mary Lee can bear witness."

"He did."

The only thing Homer loves more than Lonnie is chasing Rocky up trees. Rocky doesn't seem to mind it. I've even seen him cross the street to our yard, if Homer didn't come looking for him.

He didn't go up a tree tonight, though. Tonight, he went up the ladder. Up the ladder and up Lonnie and on up the roof.

Leona shrieked and we followed her out. The gawkers closest to the action ran around the house to see what was happening.

"Lonnie? Hon? Are you all right?"

"I'm fine, but that crazy cat's up here. Tiny, dang it, take that hell-hound home."

Maybe Rocky didn't like the heavy-duty hiss of the blower, or maybe he was scared of that giant red thing on his roof, or maybe he was mad because he wasn't up a tree. Whatever it was, he let out a kind of crooning yowl and kept it going pretty steady, apart from when he stopped to draw breath.

Lonnie, Me, and the Blowed Up Santa

Lonnie joined the concert, going, "Hush, Rocky. Hush, Rocky. Hush, Rocky. Hush, Rocky." With Homer's barking giving it a beat, you could have danced to it.

I got hold of Homer's collar and escorted him back across the street and put him in the house. The back gate was still locked, so don't ask me how he got out. Should have named him Houdini.

Santa was looking good and full by this time. Maybe a little tight in the belly, in fact. What was Lonnie doing?

I could hear the cheering all the way over on my sidewalk. It spread through the spectators and car-riders: "He saved the cat!" "The cat's okay!" "The cat's off the roof!"

That was when Jolly Old St. Nick blew a gasket and went *kablooie!* The Baby Jesus ball must have popped, too, because glitter flew out and flittered down, shimmering in the streetlights and the Christmas twinkle-lights.

Lonnie and me had some fun, after the shock wore off, asking each other if we'd found Jesus, but we never did.

At the time, when Santa Clause exploded, my heart like to stopped. I could imagine Lonnie jerking back and going off the roof, just like he was always scared would happen.

I shoved my way through the crowds, across the street to Lonnie and Leona's back yard.

He stood safe on the ground, in the middle of a crowd, his eyes big as golf balls, his mouth open with the corners turned down almost to his chin. "Leona's Santa! He's blowed to Kingdom Come!"

I patted him on the shoulder.

"I'll go up and turn the blower off, buddy."

He nodded, gulped, and said, "Thank you."

When I came back down, Leona had come back out from stowing Rocky away and everybody at once was telling her about the explosion.

~*~

110

"I don't blame you, Tiny," Leona said.

The television people hadn't stopped by, and Leona hadn't invited anybody in. All the excitement had made Lonnie and me hungry, so none of that good food was going to waste. I felt like the whole disaster was my fault for not putting Homer in the house in the first place. If he hadn't of chased Rocky onto the roof, Lonnie wouldn't of got distracted and let the pump go too long. I offered to pay for a replacement Santa, but Leona wasn't having any of it.

"It was a judgment on me for wanting that worldly thing in the first place," said the lady with the first dishwasher on the block. "Just sticking a Jesus in his hands didn't make him any less worldly. I should have known better. I'm just glad Lonnie's all right. And Rocky." She squeezed Lonnie's hand. "My hero! Brought him down just like a fireman."

Lonnie said, "He was walking on me, the same way he got up, and he got his claws caught in my coat. I had to ease down the ladder before he jerked me off the roof sideways. I don't hardly think that's how the firemen do it."

She gave him a little play-slap for being so modest.

~*~

Friday came, and our phone rang. I answered.

Leona said, "Are you watching the news? Turn on The Local Beat!"

That same instant, Mary Lee yelled, "Tiny!"

"Okay," I told both women. I hung up and sat down next to Mary Lee on the couch.

The reporter said, "In our final featured neighborhood, Christmas décor was upstaged by Christmas drama, as one courageous homeowner braved the weather and sacrificed his prize inflatable for the sake of his feline friend."

A bunch of people must have sent in videos from their camera phones, because the footage was kind of choppy, picking up the picture where the light was best. The reporter narrated

Rocky being stuck on the roof, and said how Lonnie had gone up after him and had left the blower unattended just so he could carry the poor fluffy dear to safety.

The news van camera had apparently been pointing at something else when Santa went off like a rocket, because they didn't say a word about it.

"And isn't that, after all," said the reporter, "what Christmas is all about?"

Mary Lee turned off the television.

"Is it?" I said.

"Is what?"

"Is that what Christmas is all about? Backing down a ladder with a twenty-pound cat hooked onto your coat, and then your decorations blow up?"

"God bless us, every one," she said. "Let's have some eggnog."

Marian Allen

Leona, Me, and the Laundromat of the Holy Spirit

Leona and I grew up together, along with the boys we finally married, and we've always been best friends, just like our husbands are. We worked at the Dollar R Two discount store together and cried when we graduated business school and got jobs in different offices.

There were only two bones of contention between us. We've learned how to negotiate around them over the years, but there was one time early in our marriages when one disagreement led straight into the other and nearly broke us up.

First: My high school sweetheart, now my husband, was a third-string football player, who was on the team because of his size (of course, everybody called him, and still calls him, Tiny) but didn't play much because he wasn't aggressive enough. His best friend, Lonnie, was, and still is, an idiot. Lonnie's tall and skinny, with ropey muscles and the IQ of a fruit fly. Leona thinks he's funny and sweet.

Second: I was raised in a church-going family, with strong moral values and deep faith, but Leona was raised in a branch of the Baptists that probably suspected breathing was sinful. Her church wasn't mean; they were right there with whatever was needed any time anybody had a house fire or there was a tornado or whatever, but, as Tiny says, "They'll about Jesus you to death along with it."

So here's what happened.

Leona, Me, and the Laundromat of the Holy Spirit

When we were still new brides, we lived in neighboring apartment buildings so cheap they didn't have laundry facilities. The boys worked Saturday jobs so we could save up to buy houses, and on Saturdays Leona and I hauled dirty clothes down the street to the Bubble White laundromat.

One Saturday, we were passing the time by talking and laughing, as wives do, about the things our husbands did that made us crazy. After some particularly Lonnie story, I made the mistake of saying, "Well, you married the fool."

She didn't talk much for the rest of the day, and she avoided me all week. The next Saturday, she said she was going someplace else and all but shut the door in my face.

I cried so much and felt so bad, I'd have forged Lonnie's name on a PhD if it could have made it up to Leona for what I'd said.

After another week of the cold shoulder, Tiny said, "I asked Lonnie what's the matter with Leona, and he said she said Brother Pike said you're a bad influence and a tool of the devil and you're trying to break up her marriage. She's going to some church laundromat."

"Some *church* laundromat? What do they use for detergent, the blood of the Lamb?"

Tiny did that rumbly chuckle that's something between a belly laugh and a cackle. I just love that man so much. "Be nice, Mary Lee" he said. "Why don't you ask if you can go with her? It might make it up to her for you telling the truth about Lon."

So I did.

Leona's eyes lit up and she threw her arms around me and wept on my neck. "Oh, honey, I've missed you so much!"

We cried and said we were sorry, being careful not to specify what for in case it got us mad again.

The next Saturday, we were off to the Laundromat of the Holy Spirit.

All the way there, Leona burbled about it. "I asked Brother Pike if it was okay for me to go here, since it's churchy but not *our* church, and he said he thought it would be all right, as long as they didn't preach heresy and I didn't take communion. So I said I'd watch out."

I didn't remind her of what Tiny always said: "If a business makes a big show of how Christian it is, put your hand on your wallet and back away real slow. It's like calling yourself Honest John's Used Cars."

The place was pretty churchy, all right. There were crosses and pictures of blond Jesuses on all the walls, and the overhead speakers played non-stop gospel music. I liked the music; it reminded me of my great-grandmother on my father's side. I could see crosses glinting from around the other patrons' necks as they looked up when we came in. I felt like a vampire at a stake-and-mallet convention.

When we came in, the lady behind the counter called out, "Welcome back, Sister Leona! And you brought a friend! Praise Jesus!"

Leona knows my church goes for good behavior and takes it easy on flat declarations. She cut her eyes at me, but I wasn't about to say or do anything that would make her mad or hurt her feelings, so I just smiled and nodded.

The lady, whose name tag said she was Sister Angelica, came over to the machines with us. Her being there, and my being on my best behavior, meant I couldn't cuss when I saw the machines cost twice the usual.

Sister Angelica said, "Did you explain to your friend why we cost more?"

Leona cut her eyes at me again and said, "No, I didn't. I'm going to pay the extra for her, so it doesn't matter."

Sister Angelica looked me in the eye and said, "We have to pay our own way in this world, amen? The straight way isn't easy, and it costs us all our worldly goods, amen?"

I thought, *Mind your own* business. But I didn't say it.

Out loud, I said, "It's more blessed to give than to receive, so who am I to take a blessing away from my friend?"

Leona coughed, but I was locking stares with Sister Angelica and I couldn't tell if it was a laughing cough or warning cough.

Sister Angelica smiled and said, "We charge so much because the surplus goes into our mission fund, amen?"

"What's your mission?" I was partly humoring Leona, but I was partly curious. A good idea is a good idea, even if the person executing it puts your back up.

Sister Angelica smiled. "We want to build more laundromats, expand into other cities, bringing the word of Jesus to the streets, where it belongs, amen?"

Leona paused in dropping her laundry into a washer. "That's your mission?"

"Praise Jesus!"

"Your mission is to build more laundromats?"

"God is good!"

"I thought you were sending missionaries to the godless or funding a soup kitchen or something."

"Our hearts are aflame with the Holy Spirit, amen?"

"Amen," I said. "Praise the Lord! Holy is His name! Amen, sister, amen!"

Sister Angelica looked at me like I was a lunatic and went back to her counter.

I wouldn't let Leona pay for my wash.

"I'm sorry, Mary Lee," she said. "I thought they had a real mission."

"Maybe they do," I said. She looked so let down, it hurt my heart. "They do have pictures of Jesus and gospel music. So it isn't a bad place."

"Being not a bad place isn't the same as being a good place," she said. "*Not everyone who saith to me Lord, Lord, shall enter the Kingdom of Heaven; but he that doeth the will of my Father which art in Heaven*. I don't think building overpriced laundromats so you can build overpriced laundromats counts." Being a fair woman, she said, "I could be wrong."

We all had supper together that night, and Leona said, "I don't want to go to that Laundromat of the Holy Spirit anymore. Let's go back to our regular place. Is that all right with you, Mary Lee?"

"Amen," I said. "But I thought Brother Pike disapproved of me."

I could have bitten my tongue, since I wasn't supposed to know about that.

Lonnie said, "Now, who in the world ever said that?"

"I just thought it," I said.

Leona glared at Lonnie, since there was only one way in the world I could have picked up that information. "I told you not to tell!"

"I didn't tell! I never breathed a word!"

"Then how did she know?"

"Well, I told *Tiny*. Tiny, I told you that in confidence. Can't you keep a secret?"

"My bad," Tiny said, taking another spoonful of buttery mashed potatoes.

Leona was red in the face. She scooted her chair back like she couldn't decide whether to get up and run out of the room or stay put.

Lonnie said, "If I didn't of told Tiny, he wouldn't of told Mary Lee, and she wouldn't of gone to that new place with you, and you two still wouldn't be talking to each other, and you'd still be crying. So it's a good thing I told, ain't it? Ain't it? Honeybunch, ain't it?"

Leona grumbled, "You didn't think it through like that." She wiped her eyes with her napkin and said, grudgingly, "But you're right."

Lonnie took her hand and squeezed it. "You're my girl," he said, and — just for an instant — I could almost understand what Leona saw in him.

About the Author

For as long as she can remember, Marian Allen has loved telling and being told stories. When, at the age of about six, she was informed that somebody got paid for writing all those books and movies and television shows, she abandoned her previous ambition (beachcomber), and became a writer.

Marian Allen